The Office Plays

The Receptionist

The Thugs

by Adam Bock

A SAMUEL FRENCH ACTING EDITION

SAMUEL FRENCH

FOUNDED 1830

NEW YORK HOLLYWOOD LONDON TORONTO

SAMUELFRENCH.COM

IMPORTANT BILLING AND CREDIT REQUIREMENTS

All producers of *THE OFFICE PLAYS must* give credit to the Author of the Play in all programs distributed in connection with performances of the Play, and in all instances in which the title of the Play appears for the purposes of advertising, publicizing or otherwise exploiting the Play and/or a production. The name of the Author *must* appear on a separate line on which no other name appears, immediately following the title and *must* appear in size of type not less than fifty percent of the size of the title type.

For **THE THUGS:**

First Produced by Soho Repertory Theatre, Inc.,
Daniel Aukin, Artistic Director, Alexandra Conley, Executive Director
in October 2006

THE THUGS was written in the Soho Rep Writer/ Director Lab and developed in workshops at the Vineyard Theatre, JAW/West Festival at Portland Center Stage, and New York Theatre Workshop.

For **THE RECEPTIONIST:**

Originally produced by the Manhattan Theatre Club,
Lynne Meadow, Artistic Director, Barry Grove, Executive Director,
Daniel Sullivan, Acting Artistic Director 2007-08 Season,
In October 2007

Development of "The Receptionist" was supported
by the Eugene O'Neill Center
During a residency at the National Playwrights Conference of 2006
Originally developed at the Perry-Mansfield New Works Festival 2006

CONTENTS

THE RECEPTIONIST

CHARACTERS

BEVERLY WILKINS. The receptionist.
LORRAINE TAYLOR. A co-worker. Single.
EDWARD RAYMOND. Their boss. A young grandfather.
MARTIN DART. Married, with a child.

THE RECEPTIONIST was developed at the Perry-Mansfield Performing Arts School New Works Festival, June 2006 with Primary Stages. Development of *THE RECEPTIONIST* was supported by the Eugene O'Neill Theater Center during a residency at the National Playwrights Conference of 2006.

Originally produced by the Manhattan Theatre Club, Lynne Meadow, Artistic Director, Barry Grove, Executive Director, Daniel Sullivan, Acting Artistic Director 2007-08 Season in October 2007.

BEVERLY WILKINS . . . . Jayne Houdyshell
LORRAINE TAYLOR . . . . Kendra Kassebaum
EDWARD RAYMOND . . . . Robert Foxworthy
MARTIN DART . . . . Josh Charles

Directed by Joe Mantello; scenic design, David Korins; costume design, Jane Greenwood; lighting design, Brian Macdevitt; sound design, Darron L. West; casting, David Caparelliotis; production stage manager, Martha Donaldson; stage manager, Amy McCraney.

PART ONE

*(**MR. RAYMOND** sits in a chair. There is a spotlight on him.)*

MR. RAYMOND. My cousin used to take me rabbit hunting. I didn't like it. We'd be out in the woods and I'd spot one. I wouldn't want him to notice it. He used a bow and arrow. They scream. I didn't like it. Me I like fishing. I like fly fishing. There's nothing like it. I love it. I love everything about it. I love watching the line as I cast

You actually throw it back and forth and that curl of line flying out over the water it's

I'd have to show you I wish I could show you You'd love it.

I love reading the stream. Figuring out where the big boys are hanging out. And matching the hatch. And then floating my fly right to them and waiting for them to pop and grab it.

I love catching fish.

I love letting them go too.

I have a philosophy when it comes to a caught fish. If you catch a fish and it's ok, you let it go. But if it's snagged or it's got a hook in its gills you can't put it back in the stream because it'll die. So if that happens I think you should prepare the fish to be killed.

What I do

I bleed the fish It seems a bit gruesome but I cut the gills and I hold it in the water of the stream and bleed it out. It's the humane way to kill a fish. It depletes its oxygen levels and it goes to sleep. And then I eat it. And that's ok. Because everything out there is eating something.

But if I can I let them go.

My wife doesn't fish. She spends her time thinking about the Which I understand. She sees pictures of the people over there and what we're doing to them and she cries. I keep telling her "Don't look at those pictures."

We have friends whose kids are over there. We gotta believe we're doing the right thing. But she

I don't like thinking about it. It makes me sad. It's like we're all trapped in a

When things are hard I think about fly fishing.

Ok so. Let's give this another try.

(He stands.)

PART TWO

(The reception area of an office. The receptionist's desk. Does it have tall front? Perhaps we can only see her shoulders and her head when she sits down? Or is it an island? Chairs. A side table with magazines and flowers. There are two doors upstage to **LORRAINE** *and* **MR. RAYMOND** *'s offices.*

The office is nothing special.

BEVERLY *is on the phone with her friend Cheryl Lynn.)*

(Author's note: **BEVERLY** *is listening to a long story. About a trip Cheryl Lynn took down to the shore. Where Cheryl Lynn went to the beach. And she met a man from Flom, Minnesota. Who might have a gambling problem. But Cheryl Lynn didn't know that until later. They went to the casino. He won $175,000 at blackjack. He was playing two tables at once. Making $2,500 bets. And Cheryl Lynn was standing next to him. And one time he got so excited, he put his hand on Cheryl Lynn's breast. And Cheryl Lynn was so shocked, she let him. And then they went to a very fancy restaurant named, what was it called? Timbuktoo. I think. And then he mentioned his wife. And that he couldn't tell his wife he was at the casino. Or even at the shore because she'd know he was at the casino.*

And then **BEVERLY** *gets another call. And so on.)*

BEVERLY. Which one did you go to?

Oh. Oh. I've heard that beach is so

Uhm.

Uhm.

Was he from Minneapolis? Where? Where? How'd you meet him?

Cheryl Lynn! You're a bad girl!

(Laughs.)

Uhm.

WHAT. WHAT. Oh my gosh. WHAT. He did not.

Ok that's

What did you have? He paid right?

He is? You make me crazy He's married? He's married.

Cheryl Lynn.

Uh huh.

Uhm.

He's married Cheryl Lynn!

Honestly he's

It's ok for

Just give me a second. I have a call.

Northeast office.

Oh hey Sandra. How are you? No He's not in at the moment, can I put you into his voicemail? Ok. Here you go.

Cheryl Lynn? I'm back. Listen.

No really It's ok for

Awch. Give me another second I have a call. I know, right?

Northeast office.

I'm sorry He's not in at the moment Can I put you into his voicemail?

He's not in. Can I

Yes. I can't help you with that. Can I put you

I understand. But he's not in.

I can't help you with that. I'm going to I'm going to put you into his voicemail. Ok. I'm sorry.

Cheryl Lynn? I'm back.

Oh good god

Just

Northeast office.

I'm. His voicemail is all I can

I can take your name and and

He's out so I can't.

He's out of the office. He is. He's out. Well I'm sorry but. Would you like to leave your name with me?

Ok. Ok. I'm sorry.

Cheryl Lynn? I know.

So

Let me just say this

It's ok for Maureen to go out with married men. It's not ok for you to.

Because she's stupid. I'm not being mean.

But she

(**LORRAINE** *enters.*)

Oh Just a Morning Lorraine.

LORRAINE. My bus was late again. Is Mr. Raymond in there?

BEVERLY. He's out on a visit.

LORRAINE. Oh good. Oh good. My bus was so late. And I was late for my bus in the first place so. I kept looking at my watch and I knew I. He's out?

BEVERLY. Yes he

LORRAINE. I'm just going to drop my coat.

(*Goes into her office.*)

BEVERLY. (*To Cheryl Lynn.*) Sorry That was Lorraine. She's late. Again. It's her bus.

(*Laughs.*)

I know. It's always her bus. "My bus was late."

Right!

(*Laughs.*)

So listen.

LORRAINE. (*Enters.*) I went out last night. Like you told me. To a club.

BEVERLY. (*To Cheryl Lynn.*) I gotta hang up. Ok.

(*To* **LORRAINE.**)

You did?

LORRAINE. Yeah.

BEVERLY. Did you have any fun?

LORRAINE. Well.

BEVERLY. Where'd you go?

LORRAINE. I went with my friend Brenda.

BEVERLY. The one with the

(*Gestures: Tongue-piercing?*)

LORRAINE. We took her car. So I was stuck there until she wanted to leave. Which was fine but then she didn't want to leave because she met this guy named Tony who owns a pool-cleaning company. He had a tattoo of a rhinoceros on his shoulder.

BEVERLY. Uh huh.

LORRAINE. And Brenda has one of those anarchist symbols on her shoulder so she said to me "Isn't that cool we both have tattoos on our shoulders" and I was like "Ok" and so she started talking to him and then talked to him and talked to him and I was sitting there and then Glen was there.

(*Opens eyes wide.*)

BEVERLY. (*Opens eyes wide.*)

LORRAINE. I know.

BEVERLY. Wanna cup of coffee?

LORRAINE. So I was "Brenda, Glen's here." "Glen's here!" And pool guy was "That Glen there? He's a prick." and I'm "I don't want to talk to pool guy about Glen, Brenda" and Brenda's "His name's not pool guy it's Tony." And I'm "Brenda!" and I start crying.

BEVERLY. Oh no. Lorraine.

LORRAINE. Glen was there.

(*Awkward pause.*)

I know.

(Long sigh. Picks up a magazine from coffee table.)

BEVERLY. My friend Cheryl Lynn picked up some guy at the beach and he won $175,000 in a casino.

LORRAINE. Lucky.

BEVERLY. Northeast office.

(Gestures "Do you want to take this call?")

LORRAINE. *(Gestures "No.")*

BEVERLY. She's not at her desk. Can I put you into her voicemail? Ok, here you go.

LORRAINE. Do you think he's a narcissist?

BEVERLY. Northeast office. She's not at her desk, can I put you in her voicemail? Oh hi Brenda.

LORRAINE. *(Gestures "No.")*

BEVERLY. How're you doing?

(Long story.)

Oh Uh huh.

What kind of pool? Oh pool pools. He cleans pools? Uh huh.

(Gestures "Wrap it up." Rolls eyes.)

Oh I have another call. I'll tell Lorraine you called. Ok. Ok.

Lord.

LORRAINE. She's really nice. Mostly.

BEVERLY. He was from Flom. A town in Minnesota called Flom.

LORRAINE. Who?

BEVERLY. Cheryl Lynn's guy The guy who won all the money. He was from a town called Flom. Who'd name a town that? Flom. Flom. Flom. "I'm from Flom. Minnesota."

LORRAINE. Maybe it's a Norwegian name. There are lots of Norwegians in Minnesota.

BEVERLY. Maybe.

LORRAINE. And lakes.

BEVERLY. It didn't sound like he was Norwegian.

Do I think who's a narcissist?

LORRAINE. Glen.

BEVERLY. Well of course he is. Lorraine.

LORRAINE. Really?

BEVERLY. Lorraine.

LORRAINE. Really?

BEVERLY. Glen? Your Glen? Come on.

LORRAINE. That's what the pool guy said.

BEVERLY. The pool guy was right.

LORRAINE. They worked together sometime when Glen was living back at his parents or maybe they were on some sports team together or maybe both The pool guy was kind of talking to me over his shoulder and I was crying a little and he said that He said "That guy's a total narcissist." And then he and Brenda drove me home.

BEVERLY. My girlfriend Georgia had a book she showed me It was called "HELP! I'm in Love with a Narcissist!" It's all about guys like Glen. The whole world revolves around them and you're just caught up in the whirlwind of it all.

LORRAINE. That sounds like me and Glen.

BEVERLY. I thought of you when I was looking through it.

LORRAINE. He's a stinker. He's not even that attractive.

BEVERLY. That's what the book said. They don't have to be.

Northeast office.

Oh hey Sandra. He's still not back yet. No, she's not at her desk at the moment. I know. I know. Whose voicemail do you want? Ok doll here you go.

She is such a pest!

LORRAINE. What was that book called?

BEVERLY. "HELP! I'm in Love with a Narcissist!"

LORRAINE. "HELP!"

BEVERLY. "I'm in Love with a Narcissist!"

LORRAINE. "HELP!"

BEVERLY. Yeah.

LORRAINE. I should get it.

BEVERLY. You should.

(Silence. They look off, thinking.)

Something went wrong yesterday. With a client. Mr. Raymond came back to the office very upset. He said something about letting a fish go. And he

LORRAINE. Really? Where was I?

BEVERLY. You were out.

LORRAINE. Oh.

Ok. So I better.

*(**LORRAINE** exits to her office. **BEVERLY** busies herself with office work. Nothing much. **LORRAINE** reenters.)*

LORRAINE. Glen was wearing that pair of glasses I helped him pick out.

BEVERLY. I just got started working Lorraine.

LORRAINE. Oh. Ok. Sorry.

*(**LORRAINE** exits into her office. **BEVERLY** sits. Then:)*

BEVERLY. Hi. I need to order a cake. A birthday cake. For tomorrow. Hi. Yeah. For tomorrow. Chocolate. Chocolate chocolate I guess. Do you have chocolate raspberry? Oh. Well then chocolate chocolate I guess then. Small! We don't need a big one. I'd eat it!

(Laughs.)

I'll pick it up tomorrow. How much will it be? Ok that'll be fine. Charge it to account number 637B6. Yeah Beverly. Hi. Can you write Happy Birthday on it? No, no name That'd be No Happy Birthday'll be enough that'll be fine. Ok. I'll pick it up tomorrow. Morning. Ok. Morning. Ok. Thanks.

*(**LORRAINE** enters, gets file from cabinet.)*

Here's the card I got for Mr. Raymond For his birthday. It's cute.

LORRAINE. (*Reads.*)

BEVERLY. Isn't that? (*Laughing.*)

LORRAINE. I like the little pony.

BEVERLY. I saw that and I laughed and laughed and laughed. In the store! A pony with a pipe! People are crazy!

LORRAINE. Yeah.

BEVERLY. Well go ahead and sign it. So Glen was wearing the glasses you made him buy?

LORRAINE. He'd never wear them when he was with me. He said they made him look superfluous. Remember? Remember how I told him I didn't understand what he meant by that and he ripped my coat?

BEVERLY. I do.

LORRAINE. Superfluous. I still don't understand what he was

BEVERLY. Oh don't be stupid Lorraine. He didn't know what the word meant.

LORRAINE. You think?

BEVERLY. Of course. Don't take my pen.

(**MR. DART** *enters.* **LORRAINE** *sees him.*)

LORRAINE. Ok um.

(*She hurries into her office.*)

BEVERLY. Can I help you?

MR. DART. Hello. Um. I'm here to see Mr. Raymond.

BEVERLY. Oh. Well he's out at the moment. Did you have an appointment?

MR. DART. Mindy says hello.

BEVERLY. Who?

MR. DART. Oh I'm sorry I'm Martin Dart I'm from the central office.

BEVERLY. Oh well hey Mr. Dart.

MR. DART. Mindy's our receptionist.

BEVERLY. That Mindy! At the central office!

I like her so much! I talk to her on the phone all the time. She has the cutest voice! "Central office!" "Central office!"

MR. DART. There's something Something happened to her nose. She's had a bunch of operations on it.

BEVERLY. Oh.

MR. DART. She still It's

BEVERLY. Oh.

MR. DART. Yeah.

BEVERLY. Oh.

MR. DART. I think maybe she fell.

BEVERLY. I think she has the cutest little voice. I love how it sounds.

MR. DART. Mr. Raymond is coming back today?

BEVERLY. Northeast office.

Oh hi sweetheart.

(Gestures "Can you give me a minute?")

Uh huh? Oh. Oh. Well Oh. Janey. Janey don't get worked up. Because it'll work out. You're a smart girl and they know that and

Oop Call Janey Just a

Northeast office Can you please hold?

It'll work out.

Uhm.

No because. It'll work out sweetheart. Listen. Just a second. I can't talk right now but Yeah but but Call Dad. He'll. Yeah. And then call me after you've. Ok. Call Dad and then call me ok? Ok. It'll work out. Ok. Bye Janey.

Northeast office. Sorry to make you hold. Can I say who's calling? Just a second. Lorraine, a Mr. Andrews for you? Ok.

Sorry about that. My daughter was

MR. DART. No it's ok. Family's.

BEVERLY. It is.

MR. DART. It is. It's important.

BEVERLY. She's She was all worked up.

MR. DART. It's important.

BEVERLY. Kids get worked up.

MR. DART. I have a son.

BEVERLY. You do?

MR. DART. He's four.

BEVERLY. They're so cute at that age.

MR. DART. *(Gets out his phone.)* Lemme This is

BEVERLY. He's cute. He's cute.

MR. DART. He eats paste. At preschool.

BEVERLY. That's ok.

MR. DART. You think so?

BEVERLY. Yup.

MR. DART. Really?

BEVERLY. I know so.

MR. DART. His teacher keeps mentioning it.

BEVERLY. Janey's cousin Monroe used to eat paste. He's a rock climbing instructor now.

MR. DART. Really?

BEVERLY. Uh huh.

MR. DART. Oh. Huh. I'll tell my wife. She's all worried.

BEVERLY. And he has his own apartment. He owns it.

MR. DART. I'll tell her.

BEVERLY. Tell that teacher.

MR. DART. I will.

BEVERLY. Tell her to stop scaring you. He's four! Everyone eats paste.

MR. DART. Any idea when Mr. Raymond'll be back?

BEVERLY. Soon I think Soon. He usually calls in if he's delayed. Do you want me to tell him you dropped by?

MR. DART. I'll wait for him.

BEVERLY. Oh ok.

MR. DART. I'll just wait.

BEVERLY. Ok.

MR. DART. Over here's ok right?

BEVERLY. Sure.

Do you want a cup of coffee?

MR. DART. Oh No thanks. Thanks.

BEVERLY. Northeast office.

Hi Sandra. Give me a second and I'll see if she can take your call. Hi Lorraine? Have you got time for Sandra? Ok. I'm going to put her through to you. Sandra, here's Lorraine.

*(*MR. DART *and* BEVERLY *sit. Then:)*

BEVERLY. Mr. Raymond's a really good boss.

MR. DART. Is he?

BEVERLY. He's very considerate.

MR. DART. Oh.

BEVERLY. Yup.

MR. DART. Do you have an extra pen I can

BEVERLY. Of course. You can use any of

MR. DART. Ok how about

BEVERLY. The superfine point Flexor. That's a good pen.

MR. DART. Is it?

BEVERLY. That is a good pen.

MR. DART. Huh.

BEVERLY. Yup.

MR. DART. Well alright then.

BEVERLY. And popular. Make sure you give that back to me. People keep stealing my pens. And my highlighters. I can never hold onto them. Highlighters especially. And those Flexors. They walk out of here. I had to put a lock on the supplies drawer. Lorraine would walk away with a three-hole punch if I didn't have eyes like a hawk.

I used to have three people working under me.

MR. DART. You did?

BEVERLY. Before I came to this office. I've been here for more than two years. I like the people but the office. This chair is terrible. It's. But I don't dare ask for a new one. I should have asked Steve but they reassigned him before I. And I don't dare ask the new person. Randy I think? Because I don't want to be a person who makes a fuss.

And there should be a window. It looks bare, doesn't it. That's why I bring in the flowers. They cheer the place up.

MR. DART. They do.

BEVERLY. There's no reason for it to look like a funeral parlor in here. The carpet is terrible. Isn't it? Not my colors really. But. Not much I can do.

And I came in yesterday and there were five jams in the copier. Five! Five! Someone just left it like that. Can you? It was probably Lorraine. The copier can be overwhelming.

I'm supposed to get two breaks a day. But I don't take them. I like to work. I'm a worker. My last office, everyone got let go. Except me. I got reassigned. I have a talent that way. Or a curse. Or a talent.

(Laughs.)

I got moved here. What do you do at the central office?

LORRAINE. *(In the doorway of her office.)* Beverly do you
　　Oh excuse me I didn't mean to interrupt.

MR. DART. Oh no Don't worry

LORRAINE. Sorry

MR. DART. No no

BEVERLY. Do I what?

LORRAINE. What?

BEVERLY. What.

LORRAINE. I'm Lorraine Taylor. Are you waiting to see me?

BEVERLY. He's waiting to see Mr. Raymond.

LORRAINE. Oh ok. Um.

(Goes to the files then turns back.)

BEVERLY. I'm Lorraine Taylor. I work with Mr. Raymond. Maybe I can help you? Mr?

MR. DART. Martin Dart.

BEVERLY. He's from the central office.

MR. DART. I'm from the central office.

LORRAINE. You are?

MR. DART. I am.

BEVERLY. He is.

MR. DART. I am.

LORRAINE. Do you know Mindy? "Central office." "Central office."

BEVERLY. She hurt her nose. That's why she talks that way.

LORRAINE. You must know her. She's your receptionist.

MR. DART. I do.

LORRAINE. Oh course you do. Um.

BEVERLY. Did you need something Lorraine?

LORRAINE. Oh um yeah. I need a couple of those good pens.

BEVERLY. Flexors?

LORRAINE. The pointy ones. With the

BEVERLY. I just gave you a box of them last week.

LORRAINE. What?

BEVERLY. I just gave you a box of

LORRAINE. That couldn't have been last week.

(Laughs.)

BEVERLY. I wrote it down on my calendar. See. Box Flexors L. L is for Lorraine. Last week.

LORRAINE. Well anyway. I need a pen.

BEVERLY. Uhm.

LORRAINE. I need a pen.

BEVERLY. And you looked in your desk.

LORRAINE. I need a pen Beverly.

MR. DART. I'm done with this one.

LORRAINE. I can't take your pen.

MR. DART. No it's from.

BEVERLY. Don't take the man's pen Lorraine. I'll get you a pen.

MR. DART. I insist.

LORRAINE. Well ok then thank you very much. Ok.

BEVERLY. I'll get you a pen.

LORRAINE. No need. Thank you Mr. Dart.

MR. DART. You're certainly welcome.

LORRAINE. *(Whispered to* **BEVERLY***:)* He's handsome. Find out if he's married.

BEVERLY. He is.

LORRAINE. How do you know?

BEVERLY. He has a son. He showed me his picture.

LORRAINE. Maybe he's divorced.

BEVERLY. Lorraine.

LORRAINE. Look at him looking at me.

BEVERLY. He's looking at his watch.

LORRAINE. He's sneaking looks at me. I'm going to wink at him.

BEVERLY. Don't.

> *(***LORRAINE** *does.)*

> Oh Lorraine.

> *(***MR. DART** *laughs.* **LORRAINE** *laughs.)*

MR. DART. You just winked at me.

LORRAINE. I did.

BEVERLY. She did.

LORRAINE. I did.

MR. DART. Why'd you do that?

LORRAINE. I felt like it. I like to make a little joke every now and then.

BEVERLY. She's the office joker.

LORRAINE. I am.

BEVERLY. She has to be. Otherwise it'd have to be me or Mr. Raymond and he's not funny.

LORRAINE. I get bored. Jokes liven a place up. Otherwise it can get dreary around here.

(**MR. DART** *winks at* **LORRAINE.** *She winks back. Again. Again. Again. Fun. They laugh.*)

LORRAINE. Right?

(*They wink again.*)

BEVERLY. Can you watch the phones? I'm going to get the mail.

LORRAINE. Of course I can.

BEVERLY. And stop bothering him.

MR. DART. She's not bothering me.

BEVERLY. Don't bother him.

LORRAINE. I won't. I won't. I won't.

BEVERLY. Don't.

LORRAINE. You want me to watch your desk or not?

BEVERLY. Don't let her bug you.

LORRAINE. Beverly!

MR. DART. I won't.

LORRAINE. Beverly. Jeez.

BEVERLY. You need anything from downstairs?

MR. DART. No. Thanks.

LORRAINE. You could pick me up a croissant.

BEVERLY. I'm not letting you get crumbs all over my desk.

LORRAINE. I'll eat it in my office. I'll
    No it's ok.

BEVERLY. What kind of croissant.

LORRAINE. No it's ok. It's ok. Get the mail.

BEVERLY. Ok.
    Let me get that.

LORRAINE. I can get it I can get it. Get out of here.

BEVERLY. Ok.

> (**BEVERLY** *exits.*)

LORRAINE. Northeast office.
Oh hi Brenda.

> (*To* **MR. DART**.)

It's my friend Brenda.
Hi Brenda. Yeah I was just about to call you back but
I have to cover the phones for Beverly. Can I call you
later?
I'm fine.

> (*Almost cries.*)

No I'm fine. "HELP! I'm in Love with a Narcissist!"
It's It's a book Beverly told me about it. I'll call you.
Later. Ok? Later. Ok. Ok. Bye.

> (*Almost cries. Blows her nose.*
>
> *Awkward pause.* **LORRAINE** *looks off.*)

LORRAINE. Answering the phones can be really stressful.

MR. DART. I imagine.

> (*Awkward pause.*)

LORRAINE. I don't know how Beverly does it all day long.
I'd go crazy. "Northeast office Northeast office Northeast office" all day long!

MR. DART. Me too.

LORRAINE. Constant interruption. Phone phone phone
people like you walking in. More phone calls.

MR. DART. I'd be

LORRAINE. Right?

MR. DART. What what what?

LORRAINE. "Hello." "Hello."

MR. DART. "Hold please."

LORRAINE. Over and over and over and

> (**MR. DART** *laughs.*)

LORRAINE. I'd snap.

MR. DART. I'd be

LORRAINE. I'd snap. Totally.

(**MR. DART** *laughs.*)

LORRAINE. Right?

MR. DART. Totally.

LORRAINE. I'd be "Can someone else please answer the phone!"

MR. DART. Yeah.

LORRAINE. "Someone!"

MR. DART. "Anyone!"

LORRAINE. "Anyone!" "Please!"

MR. DART. Yeah.

LORRAINE. I'd get fired.

MR. DART. Yeah.

LORRAINE. So fast.

MR. DART. They wouldn't fire you.

LORRAINE. They totally would.

MR. DART. No way.

LORRAINE. They'd be "She just stopped answering the phones!" "All of a sudden!"

MR. DART. "She left her post!"

LORRAINE. "She abandoned the phones!"

MR. DART. They'd never fire you.

LORRAINE. I'd be out.

MR. DART. You're too pretty.

LORRAINE. Shut up.

MR. DART. You are. You are.

LORRAINE. Shut up.

MR. DART. You're a very attractive woman.

LORRAINE. Mr. Dart.

MR. DART. Martin.

LORRAINE. Mr. Dart.

MR. DART. You are. You gotta know that.

LORRAINE. You can't say things like that at the office.

MR. DART. This isn't my office.

LORRAINE. You could get into so much trouble.

MR. DART. What Are you going to

LORRAINE. What?

MR. DART. Are you going to get me into trouble?

LORRAINE. I might.

MR. DART. You might?

LORRAINE. I might.

MR. DART. You might huh?

LORRAINE. Maybe.

Northeast office.

I'm sorry he's out of the office. Can I put you into his voicemail? Ok. Thanks.

MR. DART. What kind of trouble?

LORRAINE. You're a flirt.

MR. DART. Flirting livens a place up.

LORRAINE. Does it ever.

MR. DART. No harm in it.

LORRAINE. Well.

(**MR. DART** *smiles.*)

LORRAINE. I don't know about that.

MR. DART. No harm done.

LORRAINE. It can get people into trouble.

(**MR. DART** *smiles.*)

LORRAINE. No but real trouble.

MR. DART. Lorraine it's ok. Don't worry. I'm not going to

LORRAINE. Not going to what?

MR. DART. Anything.

LORRAINE. Oh.

MR. DART. Why? Should I?

LORRAINE. Oh.

MR. DART. Because I could.

LORRAINE. It's

MR. DART. Because I would.

LORRAINE. I'm

MR. DART. I wouldn't mind.

LORRAINE. (*Mutters:*) "HELP. I'm in Love with a Narcissist!"

MR. DART. What?

LORRAINE. Nothing.

MR. DART. What?

>   (**BEVERLY** *enters. She has the mail.*)

BEVERLY. What.

LORRAINE. What?

MR. DART. What?

BEVERLY. What?

LORRAINE. There weren't many calls.

BEVERLY. Uh hm.

LORRAINE. Mr. Raymond didn't call.

BEVERLY. Ok.

LORRAINE. He didn't call I thought he would But he didn't. I thought he would.

>   (*Laughs.*)

BEVERLY. I brought you a croissant.

LORRAINE. I'm going to go do some work.

BEVERLY. Do you still want it?

LORRAINE. What?

BEVERLY. I bought you this.

LORRAINE. Oh Thanks.

BEVERLY. You're welcome.

LORRAINE. Thanks.

>   (*Exits into her office.*)

BEVERLY. So are you married?

MR. DART. I am.

BEVERLY. Uhm.

>   Ok.

(Makes a call.)

Hi Honey. Did Janey call you? Oh good. She ok? Uhm. Uhm. Oh good. Oh good. I knew you could Good. Good. Ok. Oh it's fine. I just wanted to make sure Janey. Good. Ok.

What? I thought we talked about not buying that one. We did. We did. We decided not to. Yes. We did. Bob. Yeah well.

Did you pay the phone bill? And there we go. Again! Again! Again Bob! Cause they're going to charge us another fee! I'm really mad. Well because. We.

I'll see you tonight. No. Bye.

She's ok.

MR. DART. Good.

BEVERLY. Her dad's really good at calming her down.

MR. DART. Sounds like.

BEVERLY. Ok. Good. Ok.

My husband and I. We. Do you collect anything?

MR. DART. What do you mean collect?

BEVERLY. You know collect collect.

MR. DART. Like stamps?

BEVERLY. Or anything?

MR. DART. No. Why?

BEVERLY. Oh. We do. I'm a We're collectors.

MR. DART. What do you collect?

BEVERLY. Teacups.

MR. DART. Really?

BEVERLY. They're very collectable.

MR. DART. How many do you have?

BEVERLY. Hundreds.

MR. DART. Hundreds! Hundreds?

BEVERLY. Yup.

MR. DART. Really?

BEVERLY. We have them from everywhere. From England.

And Japan. And Canada. Even.

And from here of course. Although I prefer coffee myself. To drink.

(Laughs.)

MR. DART. You collect coffee cups too?

BEVERLY. No. No. Coffee mugs How awful. No. No. Northeast office.

Hey Mr. Raymond. Uhm. Uhm. Ok. I'll tell her.

(Calls **LORRAINE.***)*

Lorraine? Mr. Raymond's been delayed. Yes. Ok.

(To **MR. DART***:)*

I should have let you talk to him. I'm

MR. DART. When's he coming back?

BEVERLY. Soon he said.

MR. DART. Oh.

Hm. Hm. Hm. Ok.

Figure I have time to get a paper?

BEVERLY. I could have picked one up for you.

MR. DART. Some air'd be nice. You need anything? Think Lorraine needs anything?

BEVERLY. Oh no thank you. How nice of you but no.

MR. DART. I'll be right back.

Hm. Ok. I'll be back. Shortly. Don't let Mr. Raymond.

BEVERLY. Ok.

MR. DART. Ok.

*(***MR. DART*** exits.* **BEVERLY** *calls* **LORRAINE.***)*

BEVERLY. He's married.

*(***BEVERLY** *hangs up.* **LORRAINE** *enters.)*

LORRAINE. Where did he go?

BEVERLY. Don't worry He's coming back. He's married Lorraine.

LORRAINE. I don't think he's happily married.

BEVERLY. He's married.

LORRAINE. You saw how he was looking at me.

BEVERLY. How could he help it? You're all

LORRAINE. What. I'm all what?

BEVERLY. Lorraine.

LORRAINE. What Beverly.

BEVERLY. You and Cheryl Lynn.

LORRAINE. What.

BEVERLY. She calls me She's all excited. "I met someone down at the shore. He took me to dinner. He's really sweet. He's from Flom, Minnesota. He's married." As if that's just another bit of the story. As if that isn't starting off on the wrong foot. As if No Lorraine. No. Because it is.

LORRAINE. Beverly.

BEVERLY. It is. Plain and simple. And it's upsetting It's upsetting! I don't
Northeast office.
Just a second. I'll see if she's at her desk.

(Phone rings in **LORRAINE***'s office.* **LORRAINE** *stays onstage near* **BEVERLY***'s desk.)*

Ok.
I'm sorry, Lorraine's not answering. Can I put you into her voicemail? Ok.

LORRAINE. I was just flirting.

BEVERLY. And my friend Anne. She's married and she's fooling around with some man she met online. I don't know what to think of you all.

LORRAINE. I was just flirting.

BEVERLY. Loyalty is Loyalty is important So important and sad when it's gone. And dangerous and sad and dangerous to throw away. To just

LORRAINE. I'm not I'm not being disloyal to anyone!

BEVERLY. You're making him be! Disloyal to his wife!

LORRAINE. Oh!

BEVERLY. "Oh!" is right. Did you think of that? Because. She'll feel it. She won't trust him and then she'll

LORRAINE. I was just flirting!

BEVERLY. And they have a four year old A little four year old boy!

LORRAINE. I

BEVERLY. She'll She'll She'll

LORRAINE. I was just flirting!

BEVERLY. Ok.

LORRAINE. I

BEVERLY. Ok.

(**LORRAINE** *sniffs.*)

Ok. I just.

I worry.

LORRAINE. I

BEVERLY. I worry that you. I

LORRAINE. I'm lonely.

BEVERLY. I

LORRAINE. I'm lonely and I miss Glen. And I know I know. I know. But I

BEVERLY. Northeast office. I'm sorry but she's not at her desk right now. Can I put you in her voicemail? Ok here you go.

You don't even know this Mr. Dart.

LORRAINE. His name is Martin.

BEVERLY. Auchht. You don't even know him. You never know who someone is until you know them. He could be anyone. And his name is Martin!

LORRAINE. So?

BEVERLY. Martin Dart. Marty. Marty Dart. Lorraine.

LORRAINE. We do too know him. He knows Mindy. He works in the central office.

BEVERLY. We don't know him.

LORRAINE. He smiled at me.

BEVERLY. You need to be more careful. Glen used to smile at you.

LORRAINE. Beverly. (*Almost cries.*)

BEVERLY. Ok. Ok. Ok. Ok. Ok.

Well. No harm done. At least you're not Cheryl Lynn. When her fellow from Flom won all that money he got so excited he put his hands right on her breasts and she was so excited she didn't notice at first. And then she noticed. And then she squealed.

LORRAINE. She did?

BEVERLY. She squealed. And they all laughed. Everyone at the table. At least you're not her. You were just flirting.

LORRAINE. I

BEVERLY. You're a good girl. No harm done.

(*Silence.* **LORRAINE** *hangs around* **BEVERLY**'s *desk. Looks at a magazine. There is a starlet on the cover.*)

LORRAINE. How am I supposed I mean look at her! She's on the cover of a magazine. She's perfect. Look at her hair! She's got someone! And they're going to get married in Fiji or Fiji! Fiji! Glen was supposed to

BEVERLY. Well

LORRAINE. I give people the benefit of the doubt. I do I do I do I believe them. A guy comes up to me and says "I'm a good guy" and I believe him! And then he isn't! but I'm already planning things and I'm confused because my sister's looking at me and my Dad's quiet whenever I mention his name

BEVERLY. Well

LORRAINE. My Dad refused to lend Glen his chainsaw! I should have known better. You'd think I'd learn. Not to trust people. I'm so stupid.

Crap.

BEVERLY. Bob spent all the money for our phone bill on a teacup.

LORRAINE. The world's a mess.

(MR. RAYMOND enters.)

BEVERLY. Oh Mr. Raymond finally!

MR. RAYMOND. Beverly Lorraine Hi.

LORRAINE. Hi Mr. Raymond.

BEVERLY. Oh good you're back. A young man has been waiting for you.

LORRAINE. Martin.

BEVERLY. Mr. Dart. But he's gone. But he'll be back.

MR. RAYMOND. Who?

BEVERLY. He'll be back.

MR. RAYMOND. Ok.

BEVERLY. Shortly.

MR. RAYMOND. I had an unfortunate afternoon. Yesterday. I broke his little finger. I thought that would do it. But

(He exits into his office.

Pause.)

BEVERLY. Yeah.

LORRAINE. Oh.

BEVERLY. See?

You can't compare yourself to someone on the front of a magazine Lorraine.

LORRAINE. She's so perfect.

BEVERLY. Those girls aren't even real.

LORRAINE. I don't have anybody. Not even Glen. I know I know. But she has everything. It's not fair.

BEVERLY. Those girls are Those girls They

LORRAINE. Look at her!

BEVERLY. It's all photographers and makeup.

LORRAINE. Yeah well.

(Pause.

MR. RAYMOND enters.)

MR. RAYMOND. Is there coffee?

BEVERLY. Yes.

MR. RAYMOND. Oh good. Lorraine. You have a minute?

LORRAINE. Of course Mr. Raymond.

(They stand at **BEVERLY**'s *desk. That moment when co-workers stand and talk at the receptionist's desk almost, but not quite, as if she weren't there.)*

MR. RAYMOND. Yesterday was

(Pause.)

They brought him in

LORRAINE. How old was he?

MR. RAYMOND. Forty-seven.

LORRAINE. Uh huh.

MR. RAYMOND. I got him set up. He'd been prepped. He hadn't slept in eleven days. The last three days he'd been on the box.

LORRAINE. Uh huh.

MR. RAYMOND. And that was after his feet'd been worked over.

LORRAINE. Right.

MR. RAYMOND. So I sized him up and I thought "This one's gonna be"

LORRAINE. Sure.

MR. RAYMOND. And I broke his little finger

LORRAINE. On his right hand?

MR. RAYMOND. Yeah.

LORRAINE. Uh huh.

MR. RAYMOND. I broke his little finger and I figured "He'll start talking" but he didn't. I was sure he
So I

LORRAINE. Did you do the wire to his eye?

MR. RAYMOND. I did.

LORRAINE. Didn't work?

MR. RAYMOND. No.

LORRAINE. No?

MR. RAYMOND. No he just

LORRAINE. Did you try both eyes? Because sometimes

MR. RAYMOND. Neither worked.

LORRAINE. Huh.

BEVERLY. Really.

MR. RAYMOND. I tried both.

LORRAINE. Uh huh.

MR. RAYMOND. He wasn't going to talk.

> I was
>
> I looked in his eyes and I thought
>
> I think I saw something and I didn't know

LORRAINE. So you went back to his feet.

MR. RAYMOND. No.

LORRAINE. You didn't?

MR. RAYMOND. No.

LORRAINE. You didn't.

MR. RAYMOND. No.

LORRAINE. Why not?

MR. RAYMOND. I don't know. I just

LORRAINE. You didn't work his feet again?

MR. RAYMOND. I saw something.

(Long pause.)

BEVERLY. Bob bought another teacup.

MR. RAYMOND. Oh no.

BEVERLY. He spent all the phone bill money.

LORRAINE. Why didn't you work his feet again? That would
be

MR. RAYMOND. I know. I just

LORRAINE. So then what did you do?

BEVERLY. Northeast office. Oh hi. Just a second.

> It's Glen.

LORRAINE. What? Who? What?

BEVERLY. It's Glen. For you.

LORRAINE. No I

MR. RAYMOND. Do you need to take that call Lorraine?

LORRAINE. No. No. Beverly I

BEVERLY. Glen? She's not at her desk. I thought she was but she must have stepped out. Would you like her voicemail? Ok.

MR. RAYMOND. I'm unsure he was involved in anything at all. They made a mistake. He shouldn't have been there.

LORRAINE. What do you mean?

MR. RAYMOND. I don't think he

LORRAINE. That's not our

MR. RAYMOND. I know that.

LORRAINE. That's not our call to make.

MR. RAYMOND. I know that.

LORRAINE. So you

MR. RAYMOND. So we brought in his wife and worked on her in front of him

LORRAINE. Uh huh.

MR. RAYMOND. But I was

LORRAINE. I don't like it when we have to do that. So you

MR. RAYMOND. But he refused Still he wouldn't tell us the truth.

He wouldn't So we were

LORRAINE. I hate it when we

MR. RAYMOND. So I stopped.

LORRAINE. What?

(Pause.)

BEVERLY. What did you stop?

MR. RAYMOND. I just

(Pause.)

MR. RAYMOND. I stopped.

(Pause.)

LORRAINE. Working on her?

MR. RAYMOND. On both of them.

> I don't think he knew anything.

> He didn't know anything.

LORRAINE. But you

MR. RAYMOND. I think someone maybe just didn't like him. Someone or. Someone. And.

> And now today I just found out he hung himself last night.

BEVERLY. Oh no.

MR. RAYMOND. Yes.

BEVERLY. Oh no.

MR. RAYMOND. Yes.

BEVERLY. That's.

MR. RAYMOND. Somehow they forgot to take his shoelaces. It was a ridiculous Such a stupid oversight. And someone will be getting a very strongly worded email from me. It's not going to be easy to pass it off as an accident. Because.

> *(Pause.)*

> Hung himself.

> *(Pause.)*

> Although It made me think It's surprising more people don't do it. There are so many little ways you can, so many things you can get your hands on. All it really takes is the nerve. Still it's always surprising isn't it. Either way. When people do or when they don't.

LORRAINE. You stopped?

> *(**MR. DART** enters.)*

BEVERLY. Oh Mr. Dart!

LORRAINE. Oh. Martin.

BEVERLY. Mr. Raymond, this is who's been wanting to see you.

MR. DART. Mr. Raymond? Great!

MR. RAYMOND. Yes.

MR. DART. I'm Martin Dart.

MR. RAYMOND. Nice to meet you.

MR. DART. I'm from the central office.

MR. RAYMOND. Oh.

MR. DART. I work with Jack Roberts.

MR. RAYMOND. Beverly didn't tell me.

BEVERLY. I didn't? Didn't I? I said Mr. Dart from the central office.

MR. RAYMOND. No.

BEVERLY. Oh. Didn't I?

MR. RAYMOND. It doesn't matter.

BEVERLY. I thought I I'm sure I

MR. RAYMOND. It doesn't matter. Beverly.
Wait a minute. I know you. I met you at the 5k run. Last May.

MR. DART. Yeah. I ran that that race.

MR. RAYMOND. That's why you look familiar.

MR. DART. That was a hard one.

MR. RAYMOND. Yeah.

MR. DART. That was a hard race.

MR. RAYMOND. It was a bit hot I think.

MR. DART. I think so.

MR. RAYMOND. A bit hot for running.

MR. DART. It was.

MR. RAYMOND. Yeah.

MR. DART. It was.

MR. RAYMOND. A lot of people were dehydrated.

MR. DART. Yeah.

MR. RAYMOND. Ok. So. Just give me a moment to finish something up and then I'll see you?

MR. DART. Ok. Sure.

MR. RAYMOND. Ok.

(**MR. RAYMOND** *goes into his office. Closes his door.*)

BEVERLY. That's so strange. I'm sure I mentioned that you were from the central office to him. Didn't I Lorraine?

LORRAINE. I'm going to do some work.

(Exits into her office.)

BEVERLY. You found a paper ok?

MR. DART. Oh yeah. At the store on the corner. They sell these pastries that are so

BEVERLY. They're good aren't they?

MR. DART. They're so good.

BEVERLY. Did you have the one with the pumpkin creme?

MR. DART. No I had this strawberry berry berry thing it was I had two of them.

*(**MR. RAYMOND** comes in from his office.)*

MR. RAYMOND. Martin? I'm ready for you now.

MR. DART. Oh good. Ok.

MR. RAYMOND. Put all my calls into my voicemail Beverly.

BEVERLY. Ok Mr. Raymond.

*(**MR. DART** exits into **MR. RAYMOND**'s office. **BEVERLY** works.)*

MR. RAYMOND. *(Offstage argument, we can't really hear it. Then we hear: Yelling, in his office. The door is shut, but we still hear.)*

That's ridiculous You know that's ridiculous You know that it's!

I won't be quiet! You know that's completely!

*(**LORRAINE** opens her door. **MR. RAYMOND** rushes towards the exit. **MR. DART** follows quickly.)*

MR. DART. Mr. Raymond.

*(**MR. RAYMOND** stops. Panicked.)*

MR. DART. Mr. Raymond. Edward. Don't.

BEVERLY. Mr. Raymond?

(Pause.)

MR. DART. I am going to go and get your coat. It's cold outside.

(**MR. DART** *goes back into* **MR. RAYMOND**'s *office.* **MR. RAYMOND** *stands.*)

BEVERLY. Mr. Raymond?

MR. RAYMOND. Please call my wife. For me. Would you do that?

BEVERLY. Mr. Raymond what's

(**MR. DART** *enters. Hands* **MR. RAYMOND** *his coat.* **LORRAINE** *stands in the doorway of her office.* **BEVERLY** *is standing at her desk.*)

PART THREE

(The next morning. **BEVERLY** *enters, carrying a cake box. Hangs up her coat. Makes the coffee. Turns on the light at her desk. Turns on her computer. Starts to turn on the phones. Then:*

LORRAINE *enters from her office. She has her coat on.)*

LORRAINE. Oh! I didn't know you were here.

BEVERLY. Morning.

LORRAINE. Hi.

BEVERLY. Hi. What are you doing here?

LORRAINE. What do you mean?

BEVERLY. You're early.

LORRAINE. I had some

BEVERLY. You never come in this early.

LORRAINE. I

*(***BEVERLY*** waits.)*

LORRAINE. My bus came on time.

(Laughs.)

BEVERLY. What?

LORRAINE. Yeah! Yeah! Yeah! I know!

(Laughs.)

I ran and then I got to the bus stop and then the bus came right up and I got on. It was weird.
Because normally I run and I just miss it every time and I'm "Oh no Oh no Oh no Beverly's gonna give me that look again She's gonna give me" and

BEVERLY. What look?

LORRAINE. This one.

(Gives her that look.)

BEVERLY. What are you talking about.

(**LORRAINE** *gives her that look. Laughs.*)

BEVERLY. I don't do that. I never look at you like that.

LORRAINE. Yeah you do. Every time.

BEVERLY. I do not. I do this.

(*Gives* **LORRAINE** *a look.*)

LORRAINE. (*Laughs.*) Yeah or that one.

BEVERLY. Or.

(*Gives her another look.*)

LORRAINE. (*Doesn't laugh.*) Don't do that one. That one scares me. I don't like that one.

BEVERLY. Yeah yeah.

LORRAINE. There are a whole bunch of weirdos on the bus. I never noticed before.

BEVERLY. I take the bus.

LORRAINE. Yeah but.

BEVERLY. You take the bus.

LORRAINE. This lady had a plastic rainhat You know one of those It's not raining today. It's not going to rain today.

The bus was fun. And I got here early!

What time does Mr. Raymond usually come in?

BEVERLY. He gets in at nine-fifteen.

LORRAINE. Oh.

BEVERLY. You beat him.

LORRAINE. He's going to be surprised.

Glen called me last night.

BEVERLY. What?

LORRAINE. Yeah. At home.

BEVERLY. Did you hang up on him?

LORRAINE. No.

BEVERLY. I would have hung up on him so fast. I would have been "Oh no. Oh no. No." and then.

(*Hangs up.*)

LORRAINE. He was "Oh it was good seeing you last night at the club" and "What were you doing there?"

BEVERLY. You tell him it was none of his business?

LORRAINE. No.

BEVERLY. I would have been "That is none of your business" and then.

(Hangs up.)

LORRAINE. Beverly.

BEVERLY. Lorraine.

LORRAINE. I didn't want to

    I

BEVERLY. How long did you talk to him for?

    (**LORRAINE.** *Snaps her fingers three times.*)

BEVERLY. How long?

LORRAINE. About an hour.

BEVERLY. An hour!

LORRAINE. Maybe

BEVERLY. An hour! An hour! An hour! I'm going to teach you how to hang up.

LORRAINE. He just started talking and talked and talked and talked and the whole time all he talked about was himself! So finally I said "Glen you're a total narcissist!"

BEVERLY. You did?

LORRAINE. Yeah!

BEVERLY. Good for you!

LORRAINE. *(Laughs.)* HELP!

BEVERLY. HELP!

LORRAINE. HELP!

BEVERLY. HELP!

LORRAINE. I was shaking my head! Jeez.

BEVERLY. And you were early. You're doing good.

LORRAINE. I'm going to learn I'm going to figure out what I'm doing wrong. Because I don't want

BEVERLY. You're a good girl and you'll meet a good guy one of these days.

LORRAINE. Because I get it.

BEVERLY. Good. Ok.

LORRAINE. You're so nice to listen to me about all this stuff. I mean I know you think I'm crazy

BEVERLY. I don't think you're crazy. I just don't think you should

LORRAINE. I know you think I shouldn't even look at him I know but you're nice to You're nice about it. I appreciate it.

(Leaving her purse on a chair, she goes into her office, taking her coat, and comes out carrying a plant.)

Here. I want you to have this.

BEVERLY. Why?

LORRAINE. I appreciate you always listening to me. And plus I'm killing it. Look. It's all sickly. You're good with plants. Plus

BEVERLY. Really?

LORRAINE. You could keep it alive.

BEVERLY. It just needs water. It's dry.

LORRAINE. See?

BEVERLY. Ok. Really? Thank you.

LORRAINE. Look at it. Sitting there it looks relieved.

What happened with the teacup?

BEVERLY. Oh. Bob. He makes me so mad. The teacup was beautiful.

LORRAINE. Was it?

BEVERLY. Yeah. We've been looking for one like it for It's a Anyway it's beautiful Gorgeous and it was very hard for me to stay mad at him but I did.

(Listens to first message.)

Huh.

I get home last night and I walk in the door and he's standing there and I'm about to let him have it but he's standing there and he has the teacup and you should see it it's beautiful

(Listens to second message.)

Huh.

The colors are so And it's in mint condition It's breath-taking It's

(Listens to third message.)

Oh.

(Listens to fourth message.)

All of these calls were from Mr. Raymond's wife. He never went home last night.

LORRAINE. What?

BEVERLY. No.

BEVERLY. *(Listens to fifth message.)* Oh. That's

LORRAINE. Did he call you yesterday? After

BEVERLY. No.

LORRAINE. He didn't call me either. And he never went home.

Did you call Mrs. Raymond yesterday?

BEVERLY. I'm calling her now.

Just a

It's their machine.

LORRAINE. Tell her that

BEVERLY. *(Leaving a message.)* Hi Mrs. Raymond. This is Beverly from the office. Mr. Raymond left the office yesterday morning to go I think to the central office and then didn't come back in the afternoon So maybe call over there? and then please give me a call? Ok. Um. Ok.

I hope he's all right. I'm going to call Mindy.

LORRAINE. No don't.

BEVERLY. Why not?

LORRAINE. I don't think we should call Mindy.

BEVERLY. Why not?

LORRAINE. I just don't think we should.

BEVERLY. Northeast office. Oh hey Sandra! How are you?

No He's not in at the moment. Can I um Can I put you into his voicemail? Ok. Here you go. Why shouldn't we call Mindy?

LORRAINE. Don't.

BEVERLY. Why?

LORRAINE. Don't.

BEVERLY. Lorraine.

LORRAINE. It's just

BEVERLY. When someone goes to the central office When someone is taken there When

BEVERLY. Like Mr. Raymond? But he

LORRAINE. Like Mr. Raymond When

BEVERLY. But he wasn't "taken" there. Was he? You think that's what happened yesterday?

LORRAINE. I think he was.

BEVERLY. Why would they take him there?

LORRAINE. I don't know.

BEVERLY. You think they kept him there overnight?

LORRAINE. He didn't go home.

BEVERLY. But

LORRAINE. I think he's in real trouble.
It had to be something to do with that client he talked about yesterday. Do we know who he was?

BEVERLY. Let me look. Mr. Raymond met with him the day before yesterday right?

LORRAINE. Yes.

BEVERLY. Let me look Let me look I'll pull up
That day he only had one appointment

LORRAINE. It had to be that guy. Because

BEVERLY. Uh huh.

LORRAINE. The file's probably in Mr. Raymond's office.

(**LORRAINE** *exits into* **MR. RAYMOND**'s *office.*)

BEVERLY. Lorraine Lorraine Get out of there Lorraine. Northeast office. I'm sorry. Lorraine. She's not at her

desk. Can I put you into her voicemail? Ok. You're welcome. Here you go. You shouldn't be in there.

LORRAINE. Do you have the key to his file cabinet?

BEVERLY. Northeast office

(To **LORRAINE.** *)*

No.

How can I help you? He's not in yet.

LORRAINE. Do you have the key?

BEVERLY. You can't go poking around in his

LORRAINE. Do you have it?

BEVERLY. Yes but

LORRAINE. Give it to me.

*(***LORRAINE** *takes the key.)*

BEVERLY. I'm going to put you in his voicemail.

LORRAINE. Watch the door for me.

*(***LORRAINE** *exits into* **MR. RAYMOND** *'s office.* **BEVERLY**
watches the door.

LORRAINE *reenters, file in hand.)*

I found it. Let's see what
(Reads it.)

BEVERLY. Give me that key back. What does it say?

*(***LORRAINE.** *Holds up hand.)*

Is there anything

LORRAINE. It looks There's It's. There's nothing unusual
about This case looks so routine.

BEVERLY. Put it back.

LORRAINE. The client was picked up because he was the
brother of a

So I don't know why Mr. Raymond would have
thought

There's nothing

I don't

You should have called Mr. Raymond's wife yesterday.

BEVERLY. Why didn't you call her?

LORRAINE. I thought you did.

One of us should have. Because if he's there, there's a good chance she's there now too.

BEVERLY. This is

LORRAINE. If we'd called her At least she would have had a choice.

BEVERLY. Lorraine.

LORRAINE. Because Mr. Raymond He would have told her Beverly "When this happens to someone you are involved with You have two options." You can run. Or you can act as if nothing's happening and sit there as quiet as a rabbit under a hedge and hope they pass you by.

Most of the time they notice you sitting there though.

BEVERLY. I wonder what he did.

LORRAINE. What if he was just tired? People get tired!

BEVERLY. He must have done something. No Lorraine He must have.

LORRAINE. We don't know that he was involved with anything.

BEVERLY. They must have thought he was or else they wouldn't have wanted to talk to him.

LORRAINE. Mr. Raymond?

BEVERLY. He acted so strange.

LORRAINE. He looked tired.

BEVERLY. No it was something

I was wondering what was He must have been doing something. And since he was doing something I'm glad they. I am.

LORRAINE. What if he didn't do anything?

BEVERLY. He must have done something. Otherwise they wouldn't have taken him to the central office.

LORRAINE. But what if

BEVERLY. No.

LORRAINE. What

BEVERLY. No.

No.

He must have done something.

LORRAINE. (*Quiet.*) Thing is Beverly I kind of understood what he was

I've seen

Every now and then someone will come through and I'm "This guy didn't do anything This guy" or "He doesn't know anything."

BEVERLY. (*Quiet.*) Lorraine.

LORRAINE. (*Quiet.*) Sometimes I think "They made a mistake."

"Here I am breaking someone's"

(*Sharp intake of breath.*)

"And this person might not even"

BEVERLY. Lorraine.

(*Pause.*)

We need to find out what people are going to do before they do it.

LORRAINE. What if.

BEVERLY. We do.

LORRAINE. I know.

BEVERLY. We have to.

LORRAINE. I know.

BEVERLY. Terrible things happen when we're too trusting.

LORRAINE. (*Very quiet.*) I know. I know.

BEVERLY. Terrible things.

LORRAINE. It's just

If you can't trust anyone, how can you trust anyone?

BEVERLY. People can get hurt. We know that. And our job is to make sure that doesn't happen. Your job.

LORRAINE. No you're right you're right you're right. We just have to

BEVERLY. That's your job.

LORRAINE. I know. You're right.

BEVERLY. You have a soft heart.

LORRAINE. I'm just upset about Mr. Raymond.

BEVERLY. It's upsetting. Put that file back.

(**LORRAINE** *does.*)

There's still a chance He'll come in and we'll find out what happened and the whole thing

LORRAINE. You're right. I shouldn't worry. I'm just

BEVERLY. You have a soft heart.

LORRAINE. I'm just I'm hungry.

BEVERLY. Did you have breakfast?

LORRAINE. No. I forgot. I was so surprised I was early.

BEVERLY. You have to eat breakfast.

LORRAINE. Yeah.

BEVERLY. You can't get by without breakfast.

LORRAINE. Maybe I'll I'm gonna run out and get a croissant.

BEVERLY. Oh Will you bring me back a bagel?

LORRAINE. Sure. What kind do you want?

BEVERLY. Go to the little shop with the smelly cheeses. And pick me up a

LORRAINE. Give me a pen, because I'll forget. I'll give you your pen back Beverly.

BEVERLY. Just a sesame bagel with a smush of But just a small smush A little chive cream cheese but not a lot.

LORRAINE. Ok.

BEVERLY. But only a smush right?

LORRAINE. Ok.

BEVERLY. Let me give you some

LORRAINE. No no don't worry it's ok. Pay me when I get back.

BEVERLY. Don't you need your coat?

LORRAINE. No. I'm just going to run. I'll be back in a sec.

BEVERLY. Just a smush.

LORRAINE. Ok ok ok.

(**LORRAINE** *exits.*)

BEVERLY. (*Turns on postage machine, then turns on Muzak. Puts a bunch of envelopes through the Pitney Bowes postage machine.*)
Northeast Office. Hey honey. So how's it going so far today? Ok good see? I told you. And your dad told you. So you just keep Good Good. I'm proud of you Janey. Ok. Good. Bye.

(**MR. DART** *enters.*)

MR. DART. Hi Beverly.

BEVERLY. Oh! Mr. Dart! You startled me.

MR. DART. Sorry.

BEVERLY. No it's. I was just.

MR. DART. Good morning.

BEVERLY. Morning.

MR. DART. How are you?

BEVERLY. Oh um. Good. Startled! But good. What I can do for you?

MR. DART. I brought you one of those pastries.

BEVERLY. You did?

MR. DART. Uh huh.

BEVERLY. Ohhhmmm.

MR. DART. With the pumpkin cream.

BEVERLY. You're a devil.

MR. DART. I thought you might be hungry.

BEVERLY. Mm. Look at this. Thank you. You didn't need to do this.

MR. DART. Is Lorraine in? I brought her one too.

BEVERLY. You just missed her. She ran out to pick me up a bagel. But I'm going to eat this instead.

MR. DART. Oh. Ok.

BEVERLY. She's going to be right back.

MR. DART. Ok. I'll wait for her. I wanted to

> *(An odd pause.)*

BEVERLY. Do you want me to give her a message?

MR. DART. No. No. I'll wait.

BEVERLY. Ok.

> *(Pause.)*

> She'll be right back.

MR. DART. How's your daughter?

BEVERLY. She's fine.

MR. DART. Everything worked out?

BEVERLY. She's fine.

MR. DART. Did she calm down?

BEVERLY. She did. This is good.

MR. DART. I just need to have a quick talk with Lorraine.

BEVERLY. Oh.

> She'll be right back.

MR. DART. I told my wife what you said about the whole paste thing.

BEVERLY. What?

MR. DART. About my son and the paste and his preschool teacher.

BEVERLY. Oh.

MR. DART. And the apartment.

BEVERLY. Oh.

MR. DART. My wife was really relieved.

BEVERLY. Good.

> *(Pause. Then:)*

> How is Mr. Raymond?

> Because.

> His wife left us a number of messages. He didn't go home last night.

MR. DART. No.

BEVERLY. Is he ok?

Where is he?

MR. DART. He's a piece of work that one.

BEVERLY. Northeast office. Oh hi Brenda. No. She just popped out. She'll be back in a moment. You want to go into her voice mail? Ok sure. Here you go. Oh I know. She told me this morning. Good for her right? I never thought she'd Right? Right! "Glen you're a total narcissist!" Right! I know! Ok so here you go. Bye. Bye.

(Pause.)

Why do you need to talk to Lorraine?

MR. DART. Mr. Raymond did something very irregular.

BEVERLY. He did?

MR. DART. How well do you know him?

BEVERLY. Why?

MR. DART. Did Mr. Raymond mention anything unusual about a client he worked on two days ago?

BEVERLY. No. No.

MR. DART. Oh.

He didn't mention anything?

BEVERLY. No. Nothing unusual.

MR. DART. Oh.

Because

Don't you need to get that?

BEVERLY. Northeast office. Uh huh. His name is Mr. Raymond. Yes. But I'm sorry he's not in at the moment. Can I put you in his voicemail. Ok. Ok. Here you go. The phones have been quiet this morning. I'm

MR. DART. Beverly Are you sure Mr. Raymond didn't mention anything?

BEVERLY. I

MR. DART. Are you sure?

BEVERLY. He was upset about something yesterday. Before you

MR. DART. Uh huh.

BEVERLY. I think he was tired. He looked

MR. DART. Something very odd happened. He stopped following the protocol. And we don't know why.

And when we talked to him yesterday, he wasn't able to tell us why. And Mr. Raymond wouldn't tell us what he knew.

BEVERLY. Maybe he didn't know anything.

MR. DART. That's what he kept saying. "I don't know anything. I don't know anything." But of course he did.

BEVERLY. Maybe

MR. DART. Of course he did.

BEVERLY. Uhm.

MR. DART. And we need to know what he knew.

BEVERLY. I understand.

MR. DART. What kind of plant is that?

BEVERLY. I don't know. Lorraine gave it to me. It was in her office forever and slowly but surely she was killing it.

MR. DART. She gave it to you?

BEVERLY. Look at it. It's in terrible

(Mr. Dart goes back into **LORRAINE***'s office.)*

Lorraine's out. Mr. Dart! Mr. Dart.

*(***MR. DART*** searches* **LORRAINE***'s office.)*

MR. DART. I'm

BEVERLY. I need to ask you to come out of there. You can't be in there when Lorraine's not here.

MR. DART. Just

BEVERLY. Mr. Dart!

MR. DART. She's not coming back.

BEVERLY. She is too. She just ran out

MR. DART. She cleaned out her desk.

BEVERLY. What?

MR. DART. All her papers are gone. Her date book's gone. And I can't find her laptop. Did you see her take it with her when she left?

BEVERLY. She's coming back.

MR. DART. No. She isn't.

BEVERLY. She didn't take her coat. She left her coat.

MR. DART. How long ago did she leave?

BEVERLY. Five minutes? Ten minutes? She's out in the cold without her coat.

MR. DART. Mindy? Hi. It's Martin. I need you to have Jack start a search immediately on Lorraine Taylor. Yes. From the Northeast office. She ran. Yes. I am. She is.

(*To* **BEVERLY***:*)

Mindy says hello.

BEVERLY. Hello.

MR. DART. Beverly says hello. Yes. Yes.

(*Laughs.*)

BEVERLY. I thought she was coming back.

MR. DART. Well.

BEVERLY. She told me she was coming back.

MR. DART. Hm.

BEVERLY. She said she was going out to get a croissant.

MR. DART. Hm.

BEVERLY. Why would she have gone?

MR. DART. Maybe you could tell me.

BEVERLY. She told me she

MR. DART. We'll find her.

BEVERLY. Lorraine is a good girl. She wouldn't be messed up in anything.

MR. DART. Yesterday you thought Mr. Raymond was a good and generous boss and now today

BEVERLY. Something must have

MR. DART. Can I borrow this pen?

BEVERLY. You can have it.

(**MR. DART** *crosses* **LORRAINE***'s name off his list.*)

Lorraine is a I've known her for two years. She would

never do anything. She would never.

MR. DART. Ok Mrs. Wilkins. Let's go.

BEVERLY. What? Where? Why?

MR. DART. I need you to come to the central office with me.

BEVERLY. Why? Go where? Why? Why?

MR. DART. We just need to talk to you.

BEVERLY. Why? Me?

MR. DART. Yes you. We need you to tell us what you know.

BEVERLY. About what?

MR. DART. We need you to tell us what you know about Mr. Raymond and his activities. And about Miss Taylor.

BEVERLY. No. Mr. Dart. No. No. Martin.

(*Laughs.*)

No.

MR. DART. We all have to do our part.

BEVERLY. No.

MR. DART. Mrs. Wilkins.

BEVERLY. Beverly.

MR. DART. Mrs. Wilkins.

BEVERLY. No. Martin. Mr. Dart. No.

(**MR. DART.** *Looks away.*)

BEVERLY. No. No. I don't know anything. I don't know anything. You know I don't know anything.

MR. DART. We find that hard to believe. You've been working here for two years.

BEVERLY. I don't know anything. I didn't do anything.

MR. DART. How

BEVERLY. I didn't!

MR. DART. How can I know you're not lying?

BEVERLY. Why would I lie? I'm not lying!

MR. DART. Yes but

BEVERLY. I'm not!

MR. DART. How can I know that?

BEVERLY. I answer the phones. That's all I do here. That's all I do.

MR. DART. You're going to have to come with me.

BEVERLY. Couldn't you let me go? I won't say anything. I.

MR. DART. Mrs. Wilkins. Let me tell you how this is going to happen. You're going to put on your coat and you are going to turn off the light on your desk and you are coming with me to the central office and there you are going to sit down with me and answer a number of questions and if you do? well then ok. And if you don't?

BEVERLY. I

MR. DART. Do you understand me Mrs. Wilkins?

BEVERLY. I

MR. DART. I know where to find your daughter Janey.

BEVERLY. You

(**MR. DART.** *Looks away.*)

BEVERLY. You

(**MR. DART** *looks at* **BEVERLY**.)

BEVERLY. You could help me.

MR. DART. Beverly. I have to ask you to get your things together.

BEVERLY. You could.

MR. DART. I don't want to meet your daughter.

BEVERLY. (*A sharp breath.*)

MR. DART. (*Looks away.*)

BEVERLY. I. I. I need to turn off the coffeemaker. And I need to water this plant. It's dry.

MR. DART. Ok.

(*He waits while she does.*)

BEVERLY. Who'll answer the phones?

MR. DART. Maybe you could leave a message?

BEVERLY. That's a good idea.

Hello. The Northeast office is closed for the day. If you know your party's extension, key it in now. Otherwise leave a message, and we'll return your call. Thank you.

(**BEVERLY** *gathers her things. Puts on her coat.*)

MR. DART. Turn off the light on your desk.

(**BEVERLY** *turns off her light. Stands.*)

MR. DART. I'm sorry you're scared.

PART FOUR

(**BEVERLY** *sits in a chair, similar to the chair* **MR. RAY-MOND** *sat in during the prologue. There is a spotlight on her. A phone rings. She is startled and looks towards the sound.*)

END OF PLAY

THE THUGS

CHARACTERS

MERCEDES. Temp. 38. Drawn.
ELAINE. Temp. 46.
DIANE. Temp. 26. Supervisor.
MARY. Temp. 45. From Maine.
BART. Temp. 37.
DAPHNE. Temp. 24.
CHANTAL. Temp. 37. New to the office.
JOEY. 26. Daphne's boyfriend.

THE THUGS was first produced by Soho Repertory Theatre, Inc., Daniel Aukin, Artistic Director, Alexandra Conley, Executive Director in October 2006.

ELAINE . . . . Saidah Arrika Ekulona
BART . . . . Brad Heberlee
DIANE . . . . Carmen M. Herlihy
JOEY . . . . Chris Heuisler
DAPHNE . . . . Keira Keeleymary
MARY . . . . Lynne McCullough
CHANTAL . . . . Maria Elena Ramirez
MERCEDES . . . . Mary Shultz

Directed by Anne Kauffman; scenic design, David Korins; costume design, Michelle R. Phillips; lighting design, Ben Stanton; sound design, Robert Kaplowitz and Jeremy J. Lee; production stage manager, Sarah Bishop-Stone.

SET

An obscure floor in a high-rise office building. Where temps do coding work for a law firm.

Onstage there are long tables. Boxes of files. Papers on tables. No computers. Coding is repetitive fact and number checking and classification.

One phone on the floor. Pencils and highlighters. There are windows upstage – a long horizontal narrow band of windows that run the length of the office. There is an elevator, with numbers that flash the floors above the door. We are on the ninth floor.

Offstage left, there is a bathroom and fire door to a stairwell down a long hallway.

Offstage right, a kitchenette.

It is gray. Inside and out. The desks. The carpeting. The light outside.

Another note:
I would suggest that the sounds and lighting in the office be treated both as background and as character.

And also:
Consider overlapping the dialogue. Often 2 or more characters should talk at once, when more than one conversation is going on.

Scene 1

(Lights come up slowly. The office. The noises in the office are at first coincidental, then slightly intriguing, then possibly ominous. A strange, natural symphony. Outside it begins to rain.

Lights go down slowly. Pale grey light to black.)

Scene 2

(Lights come up slowly. **MERCEDES** *is onstage right. Crosses. Exits stage left. Enters. Mutters.*

Elevator door opens. **ELAINE** *enters listening to her cellphone. Looks at* **MERCEDES**. *Looks away when* **MERCEDES** *looks at her.* **ELAINE** *goes and sits at her desk.)*

MERCEDES. Oh. Ah. Elaine!

ELAINE. Stt.

MERCEDES. I made coffee!

ELAINE. Mercedes.

MERCEDES. Can you?

ELAINE. No no I'm. Messages.

MERCEDES. Elaine?

ELAINE. No I'm I'm listening.

(She does.)

Ahgh. Uh. She's awful. She's.

MERCEDES. Who?

ELAINE. Oh.

MERCEDES. Who?

ELAINE. Mercedes I'm trying to.

MERCEDES. *(clucks tongue.)*

ELAINE. Don't cluck at me! I'm just! Ok?

MERCEDES. *(mutters.)*

ELAINE. It's not It's not nine yet. It's not even. So.

MERCEDES. You don't have to be.

ELAINE. I'm not being. It's not nine.

MERCEDES. Well you.

ELAINE. I'm not.

MERCEDES. You.

> *(**ELAINE** moves papers on table, to scare **MERCEDES**.)*

MERCEDES. Ok.

> *(Exits offstage left.*
>
> *Enters.)*
>
> Because.

> *(**ELAINE** turns her head away.)*

MERCEDES. Ok.

> *(Exits.)*

ELAINE. *(Makes a call on cellphone.)* Andrea? Yeah.
No. No. No. No. No. Uh uh. No.
No.
Because.

> *(**MERCEDES** enters.)*

Andrea.

> *(Elevator door opens. **DIANE** enters.)*

MERCEDES. Hi oh! Diane!

DIANE. Uh huh.

ELAINE. Oh forget it!

> *(Hangs up.)*

Hi Diane.

DIANE. Hey Elaine.

MERCEDES. Diane! I like that coat!

DIANE. Is the coffee made?

MERCEDES. I made the coffee!

ELAINE. I put the coffee on.

DIANE. Oh good.

MERCEDES. What?

ELAINE. What.

MERCEDES. Oh. That's.

DIANE. You want a cup?

ELAINE. No thanks.

MERCEDES. Diane?

DIANE. What time is it Is it nine?

MERCEDES. It's close. I think.

ELAINE. No.

MERCEDES. Isn't it?

ELAINE. Nope. It isn't.

DIANE. Oh good.

    (Exits.)

MERCEDES. Ah. I made the.

    (Blinks.)

    Coffee.

ELAINE. You calling me a liar?

MERCEDES. No! No.

ELAINE. Good because.

MERCEDES. Ah. Ip.

DIANE. *(Enters.)* What's wrong?

ELAINE. Nothing.

MERCEDES. No.

DIANE. No?

ELAINE. Nothing. My sister. My.

DIANE. What about her?

MERCEDES. My sister's taking a karate class.

    (Opens her eyes wide.)

ELAINE. My older sister.

DIANE. Your sister Teresa?

ELAINE. My goddamn sister Andrea.

MERCEDES. My sister. She's.

ELAINE. She's playing games.

DIANE. What did she?

ELAINE. She called. She gave me names of funeral homes.

DIANE. Uh huh?

ELAINE. In New Hampshire.

MERCEDES. (*Muttering.*) I love New Hampshire. I've been to Concord. It's the capital.

ELAINE. She wants me to bring my mother's body up there.

DIANE. When?

ELAINE. Otherwise "she's washing her hands."

DIANE. Really.

ELAINE. Like she's not my mother's daughter too.

DIANE. Like she could "wash her hands."

ELAINE. She's "washing her hands."

DIANE. "Washing her hands!"

ELAINE. "Washing" them!

DIANE. Right!

ELAINE. "Washing her hands!"

MERCEDES. When did your mother pass?

ELAINE. What?

(**ELAINE** *and* **DIANE** *look at* **MERCEDES.**)

MERCEDES. I'm so. Ah.

ELAINE. Just.

MERCEDES. Oh.

ELAINE. I'm.

MERCEDES. Oh.

ELAINE. I'm.

MERCEDES. I didn't know.

DIANE. So what happened?

ELAINE. So I called her back.

DIANE. When?

ELAINE. Just before you

And then she was all

*(Elevator door opens. **DAPHNE**, **BART** and **MARY** enter.)*

BART. "IT'S ALL RED! IT'S ALL RED! AND YOU BETTER TAKE IT OFF!"

That's what he was yelling he was yelling Loud Loud Hey Diane Hey Elaine Hey Mercedes. Daphne. Hey

MERCEDES. Hi Bart! Hi!

DIANE. Yeah ok.

BART. "IT'S ALL RED!"

DAPHNE. In front of her?

MERCEDES. Who?

BART. Yeah!

MERCEDES. Who?

DAPHNE. Right in front of her?

BART. Right in front of her! Yeah!

DAPHNE. No way!

BART. Yeah! Yeah! Yeah!

DIANE. Good morning Mary.

BART. She hadn't even noticed!

*(**DAPHNE** opens mouth wide.)*

BART. I KNOW! RIGHT? PAH! I know.

ELAINE. She started swearing at me. Lots of.

MERCEDES. I made coffee!

BART. Great!

So I said to her I said

*(Follows **DAPHNE** offstage right.)*

ELAINE. She was. Using words I never.

DIANE. Really?

MERCEDES. Hi Mary!

ELAINE. Words I'd never think to. With my sister!

DIANE. So you're

ELAINE. I hung up!

DIANE. Of course you

ELAINE. I hung up!

DIANE. She was swearing?

ELAINE. I hung up! Nobody's swearing at me!

DIANE. Well yeah.

(**BART** *and* **DAPHNE** *enter with coffee.*)

BART. Ok? COLLAPSED! And that was that. Coffee's good.

ELAINE. Thanks.

MERCEDES. Umph! Ah ah.

DAPHNE. I would of just smacked him.

BART. Yeah, you would of. But.

DAPHNE. Whacked him.

MERCEDES. Who?

BART. She's not like that.

DAPHNE. Knocked him on his ASS.

BART. She wears pearls.

(**DAPHNE** *laughs.*)

She's very fancy.

MERCEDES. Who?

BART. Fancy.

DAPHNE. What time is it?

BART. Fancy fancy.

ELAINE. We got a couple of minutes.

BART. Anybody hear anything?

(*All are quiet for a second.*)

BART. Anything? Anything new? Anything at all? Nothing?

MERCEDES. It's too terrible!

ELAINE. Oh god.

MERCEDES. It is. It is. I'm.

BART. It is terrible, isn't it!

DIANE. Bart.

ELAINE. Look, you got her started! *(Laughs.)*

MERCEDES. I'm.

DIANE. Oh now.

ELAINE. Only took you a second!

　　*(**DAPHNE** laughs.)*

DIANE. What time is it?

MERCEDES. I'm.

ELAINE. And she's "I'm I'm I'm!"

MERCEDES. It's not funny.

BART. No.

DAPHNE. You got an extra highlighter?

BART. No.

MERCEDES. It's not funny.

ELAINE. "I'm I'm I'm"

DIANE. Nothing's gonna happen to you Mercedes.

ELAINE. You never know!

MERCEDES. You don't!

DAPHNE. Anyone got a green one?

DIANE. Don't be silly.

ELAINE. You never know! *(Laughs.)*

DIANE. Nothing's even happening!

MERCEDES. Something's happening.

DIANE. We don't know that.

BART. So nobody's heard anything? Because

DIANE. Is it nine

BART. Because I heard

DIANE. It's nine

BART. Because I heard a little something.

MERCEDES. What?

DIANE. It's nine.

MERCEDES. What did you hear?

DIANE. It's nine. Hey.

(They start to work. In silence.)

DAPHNE. What did you hear?

DIANE. Daphne.

(They work in silence.)

MARY. Look. It's raining again.

(They work at the tables in silence. The lights go down slowly. Pale gray light to black.)

Scene 3

*(The lights come up slowly. They are all working at the tables. **CHANTAL** is at a table seated next to **DIANE**, **DIANE** is showing her how to do the job.)*

DIANE. That's right.

CHANTAL. Like this?

DIANE. Yeah. That's right.

CHANTAL. I got caught in the rain. But I don't. Ha.

DIANE. No. Put that there.

CHANTAL. Oh.

DIANE. There.

CHANTAL. Here?

DIANE. Yeah.

CHANTAL. Really?

DIANE. Yeah.

CHANTAL. Because

DIANE. Remember I told you

CHANTAL. Oh yeah. Right.

DIANE. Because

CHANTAL. Ok ok ok I

DIANE. See? Because

CHANTAL. Ok. I get it.

DIANE. Good. That's.

CHANTAL. So this one.

DIANE. Right.

CHANTAL. Right.

DIANE. Right.

CHANTAL. Can we Do any of these Do the windows open?

DIANE. No.

CHANTAL. Oh.

DIANE. Do that one.

CHANTAL. Um.

DIANE. Yup. No.

CHANTAL. Sorry.

DIANE. Put this

CHANTAL. Right. Right.

DIANE. Yup.

CHANTAL. Sorry.

DIANE. Ok.

CHANTAL. So then

DIANE. Right.

CHANTAL. Right.

DIANE. Good.

CHANTAL. And.

DIANE. Yup.

CHANTAL. Right?

DIANE. Right.

    (**CHANTAL** *laughs.*)

    And.

CHANTAL. Right.

DIANE. No.

CHANTAL. Oh.

DIANE. Because. Look, you got to remember that.

CHANTAL. Sorry.

DIANE. Right?

CHANTAL. No sorry right no sorry no.

DIANE. It's ok.

CHANTAL. Sorry.

DIANE. It's ok.

CHANTAL. Yeah.

DIANE. You're just starting.

CHANTAL. I know how to do this.

DIANE. Ok.

CHANTAL. I do.

DIANE. Ok.

CHANTAL. I mean.

    It's hot in here.

DIANE. So if you were going to finish it?

CHANTAL. I'd?

DIANE. Good.

CHANTAL. I know how to do this.

DIANE. See?

CHANTAL. I get it.

DIANE. Good.

CHANTAL. I'm

DIANE. Good. So let's take a break.

    Break.

ELAINE. Break.

BART. Oh good. Ah ah ah! You coming?

DAPHNE. Yeah. Gimme a second.

BART. I'm going to run to the.

MERCEDES. Diane?

DAPHNE. Yeah.

    (BART exits to bathroom.)

    You coming Mary?

MARY. Yeah.

MERCEDES. Diane? Can I

DIANE. Mercedes.

MERCEDES. I only need to make one call.

DIANE. Mercedes.

MERCEDES. No ok sorry yeah

DIANE. You know

MERCEDES. No no.

DAPHNE. You can use my cellphone.

MERCEDES. Really? Oh!

DAPHNE. Yeah yeah.

DIANE. I gotta take these off.

    (Takes her shoes off. Sprays them with freshener.)

ELAINE. Sore feet?

DIANE. Oh. Fhhhhh.

MERCEDES. Oh Daphne you're

DAPHNE. Yeah. Ok.

MERCEDES. What do I?

DIANE. I dunno. They get sore.

DAPHNE. You push this. But you should go outside.

MERCEDES. Oh. Really. Oh. Oh.

DAPHNE. The signal's sort of.

MERCEDES. It's sort of?

DAPHNE. Just go out and.

MERCEDES. Oh. That's. No.

DAPHNE. It's.

MERCEDES. I'll just wait.

DAPHNE. Whatever.

MERCEDES. No.

BART. Come on.

DAPHNE. Yeah.

BART. Anyone need anything from the stinky store? You want to come?

CHANTAL. Where?

BART. To the store in the lobby downstairs.

CHANTAL. Oh thanks. No.

DIANE. No thanks.

ELAINE. Nah.

BART. No? Nobody? Ok.

(**DAPHNE, BART** and **MARY** get on the elevator.)

MERCEDES. I'll just wait.

DIANE. What're you going to do?

MERCEDES. The elevator sounds weird.

ELAINE. I'm going to call her back again.

DIANE. Hm.

ELAINE. Later.

DIANE. What're you going to say?

ELAINE. I'll figure it out.

DIANE. Hm.

ELAINE. Later.

MERCEDES. I have to put a lot of hairspray in my hair, and clips, because when the wind blows, my hair goes up.

DIANE. What do you think she'll say?

ELAINE. I dunno.

DIANE. Hm.

ELAINE. I'll figure it out.

MERCEDES. *(Sniffs.)*

DIANE. These situations are.

ELAINE. Oh yeah.

DIANE. Hm.

ELAINE. You wouldn't want to meet my sisters.

DIANE. Yeah?

ELAINE. They're both liars. Like Pinocchio.

MERCEDES. *(Sniffs.)*

DIANE. Mr. Halpert send you up here?

CHANTAL. Excuse me?

DIANE. Mr. Halpert. Did he send you?

CHANTAL. No. It was a woman.

ELAINE. Lou-Ann?

CHANTAL. Who?

ELAINE. Was it Lou-Ann?

CHANTAL. I'm sorry. I don't.

ELAINE. She have sort of a long face?

DIANE. With teeth?

ELAINE. Teeth like?

DIANE. And?

CHANTAL. She was very pleasant.

ELAINE. But.

CHANTAL. She might of been from the South?

ELAINE. Yeah. Lou-Ann.

DIANE. I wonder why Halpert didn't send her?

CHANTAL. He's not in today.

ELAINE. Really?

DIANE. Really?

MERCEDES. Huh.

CHANTAL. I was supposed to talk to him.

ELAINE. He wasn't in?

DIANE. That's weird.

MERCEDES. That is weird.

CHANTAL. That's what. Lou-Ann I guess? Said he was out.

DIANE. Really.

CHANTAL. For the day. At least for the day.

DIANE. Really.

MERCEDES. Really.

(**DIANE** *looks at* **MERCEDES**.)

ELAINE. That's weird.

CHANTAL. The whole office seemed kind of quiet.

ELAINE. How do you mean?

CHANTAL. They almost had me stay and do the phones.

ELAINE. Where was Melissa?

CHANTAL. Who?

ELAINE. The regular temp? Who does the phones.

CHANTAL. I guess she was.

ELAINE. She wasn't there?

CHANTAL. She must of been out too.

DIANE. Really.

CHANTAL. It was kind of quiet. I only saw Lou-Ann. She
      sent me up here.

MERCEDES. See?

ELAINE. See what?

MERCEDES. Nobody's coming in.

ELAINE. So?

MERCEDES. I'm going home.

DIANE. You're going home?

MERCEDES. I think. At lunch. I'm not.

DIANE. You're going home?

MERCEDES. I don't feel well.

DIANE. Huh.

ELAINE. Huh.

DIANE. You do that and you probably won't be coming back.

MERCEDES. I feel sick.

DIANE. Uh huh.

MERCEDES. *(Sniffs.)* I feel sick.

CHANTAL. None of these windows opens?

DIANE. No.

ELAINE. Besides it's raining.

DIANE. And.

ELAINE. And the papers would go everywhere.

MERCEDES. *(Laughs.)* One time!

DIANE. We keep them shut.

ELAINE. They don't open.

MERCEDES. We had a fan. (*Laughs.*)

CHANTAL. I like a bit of air.

MERCEDES. It was like a.

CHANTAL. I like.

MERCEDES. A snowstorm! But with paper.

CHANTAL. Oh.

ELAINE. Besides it's raining.

CHANTAL. Oh.

How long have you worked here?

ELAINE. Three years.

CHANTAL. Three years!

ELAINE. Diane's been here three and a half right Diane?

DIANE. Yeah.

MERCEDES. I've been here a year.

CHANTAL. Have you been working on the same case the whole time?

DIANE. No!

ELAINE. No! No! *(Laughs.)*
   I'd of gone crazy!

MERCEDES. *(Mutters. Chuckles.)*

ELAINE. That's not funny.

DIANE. That's enough Mercedes.

MERCEDES. I didn't.

DIANE. That's enough.

> (**ELAINE.** *Exits quickly to bathroom.*
>
> *Long pause.*)

DIANE. What time is it?

CHANTAL. There's a real wind out there.

> (**BART** *and* **DAPHNE** *enter off elevator.*)

BART. Stinky store is closed today. I was going to get gum but it's closed.

DAPHNE. It's got a big Closed sign.

DIANE. Where's Mary?

DAPHNE. She's still smoking.

BART. And Rick from the fourteenth floor says half his office is out.

DAPHNE. And one of the door guys isn't there.

BART. He was on his break.

DAPHNE. Was he?

BART. Yeah.

DAPHNE. He was?

BART. Yeah.

DAPHNE. Oh.

BART. Half the building's empty.

DIANE. Who told you that?

BART. They're scared.

DIANE. Who's scared?

MERCEDES. Who's scared?

> (**DIANE** *looks at* **MERCEDES.**)

BART. Lots of people.

DIANE. They are not.

CHANTAL. Why?

DIANE. They are not.

BART. *(Nonchalant.)* Someone's killing people. In the building.

Anyone have any gum?

CHANTAL. What?

ELAINE. *(At edge of stage.)* No one's killing people.

DIANE. A couple of people died.

MERCEDES. I'm I'm I'm

DIANE. Mercedes.

ELAINE. Nobody knows anything.

CHANTAL. In this building?

MERCEDES. Yes!

ELAINE. This building is huge.

DIANE. There are probably More than a thousand people

ELAINE. Probably five thousand More maybe

DIANE. Lots of people work in this

ELAINE. This building is huge.

DIANE. A couple of people

BART. That we know about.

MERCEDES. That we know about!

ELAINE. Oh don't go getting.

DIANE. We don't even know

(**MERCEDES** *opens mouth.*)

DIANE. We don't.

BART. We know something.

DIANE. Something.

BART. We do.

DIANE. We don't.

BART. We do.

DIANE. We don't.

BART. We do.

DIANE. It's gossip. It's gossip.

DAPHNE. It is gossip Bart.

BART. Two people.

DIANE. It's gossip Bart. Don't go scaring her.

BART. I'm not scaring.

DIANE. It's gossip and a lot of bored people.

DAPHNE. Where there's smoke there's fire.

BART. That's right.

DIANE. Where's Mary?

DAPHNE. She's smoking.

DIANE. Well we gotta. It's time.

> *(They work in silence.*
>
> **MARY** *enters off the elevator.)*

DIANE. You're late.

MARY. Yeah.

DIANE. Make sure you deduct it from your timecard.

MARY. Ok.

> *(They work at the tables in silence. An odd sound. They all look. They work. They work. They work. A work ballet.)*

ELAINE. *(To* **MERCEDES**.*)* My sister wants to have it up there In New Hampshire! and you You just You just You're whispering sppp sppp sppp and You're!

> *(***ELAINE*** *exits quickly to the bathroom.)*

DIANE. Elaine. *(Quickly follows* **ELAINE** *offstage.)*

> *(Silence.)*

MERCEDES. I didn't

> *(Silence.)*
>
> I
>
> *(They all look in the direction of the bathroom.*
>
> **DAPHNE** *sings a line of a song quietly.*
>
> **BART** *laughs.)*

DAPHNE. Right?

BART. So last night I saw this magician His name was Bob Bob Bob the Magician Bob the Magician so he did this trick with cards and he was moving them around shuffling them and flipping them and flipping them and like

Then all of a sudden he reached over and reached into my ear and he pulled out a snake. A live snake! Out of my ear! Yeah yeah yeah

I didn't even see him put the snake in there because I was looking at the cards! You know how he was

DAPHNE. A snake snake?

BART. Yeah! A snake snake!

DAPHNE. I hate snakes.

BART. Out of my ear.

MARY. Was it a garter snake?

BART. No It was yellow.

MERCEDES. *(mutters.)*

BART. Yeah you better believe it. You're going to be

MERCEDES. I didn't do anything. I didn't.

BART. Yeah but you're still gonna

(*DIANE enters. ELAINE stands just onstage.*)

DIANE. Mercedes.

MERCEDES. I

DIANE. I don't want to hear it.

MERCEDES. But *(Mutters.)*

DIANE. Mercedes. You need to be kinder. Or we're gonna have a I'm telling you We'll have a problem.

(*MERCEDES sniffs.*

DIANE sits down. They work.

ELAINE walks slowly to her seat. Sits down. Starts to work. The lights go down slowly. Pale gray light to black.)

Scene 4

(The phone rings. Lights come up quickly.

DIANE *answers the phone.)*

DIANE. This is Diane.

Uh huh. Both of us? Ok.

(Hangs up the phone.)

Mercedes?

MERCEDES. Yes?

DIANE. Will you come with me?

MERCEDES. Me?

DIANE. Yes.

MERCEDES. Why? Ok. Why?

DIANE. Sh. People are working.

MERCEDES. Oh.

(They get on the elevator. The others continue to work. A careful pause.)

DAPHNE. What was that?

*(**ELAINE** looks at her.)*

BART. I wonder huh.

ELAINE. There are people working.

BART. *(looks at **DAPHNE**.)* Uh huh.

DAPHNE. "Shhh."

BART. "There are people working."

ELAINE. There are.

BART. Yeah yeah Elaine.

DAPHNE. Diane's not here Elaine. You can.

ELAINE. I'm just.

DAPHNE. Uh huh.

BART. Uh huh uh huh.

DAPHNE. "Shh." "There are people working."

BART. Think she's in trouble?

DAPHNE. What'd Mercedes be in trouble for?

BART. Sounded like the office calling.

ELAINE. Halpert's out today.

BART. Oh you're not working any more?

(**DAPHNE** *laughs.*)

BART. How'd you know he's out?

ELAINE. She told us.

BART. Halpert's out?

CHANTAL. Yeah.

BART. Huh.

DAPHNE. Elaine you're gonna have to ask Diane.

BART. Yeah.

ELAINE. What?

DAPHNE. Ask her who called.

BART. You gotta find out.

ELAINE. I'm not asking her anything.

BART. You got to.

DAPHNE. You're her friend.

ELAINE. I'm not asking her.

BART. You guys are friends. It'll be easy for you.

DAPHNE. What if Mercedes got let go?

BART. That's probably.

DAPHNE. Except they would've let me go first. Or her.

CHANTAL. Why?

DAPHNE. You're new. I'm a terrible worker.

BART. She is.

DAPHNE. I am.

CHANTAL. You are?

BART. We voted. She's the worst.

DAPHNE. Overwhelmingly!

BART. Yeah!

DAPHNE. I don't like working.

BART. She doesn't.

DAPHNE. It bugs me.

BART. She has a hard time staying interested.

ELAINE. We all have a hard time staying interested. It's a stupid case.

DAPHNE. Yeah.

BART. It is a stupid case.

CHANTAL. Most of the cases I've worked on have been stupid.

DAPHNE. This one is really stupid.

BART. *(laughs.)*

DAPHNE. Wait til you get into it.

ELAINE. This one is the dumbest.

DAPHNE. Man!

ELAINE. It's dumb dumb capital d dumb.

BART. *(laughs.)*

ELAINE. Dumb lawyers saying dumb things to other dumb lawyers about dumb things stupid people did.

BART. *(laughs.)*

ELAINE. Using big stupid dumbass words! *(Laughs.)*

DAPHNE. Plus it's corrupt.

ELAINE. Well yeah.

BART. Oh and THAT. *(Laughs.)*

CHANTAL. I worked on asbestos. At my last one.

DAPHNE. You did? Defending?

CHANTAL. Yeah. Of course.

BART. Defending who?

CHANTAL. The company that installed it.

BART. Of course.

ELAINE. Of course.

DAPHNE. I heard about that gig.

CHANTAL. There were a load of us on that one. The asbestos guys had so much money Lots of money A crapload of money. The other guys don't have any money.

DAPHNE. There were lots of you on it right?

CHANTAL. They had bank.

BART. How many?

CHANTAL. Went up and down. Forty.

BART. Forty!

ELAINE. Forty!

DAPHNE. Forty temps! At once?

CHANTAL. Yeah.

BART. Forty!

ELAINE. Forty!

DAPHNE. Forty!

BART. Forty frigging temps.

DAPHNE. Fulltime?

CHANTAL. Yeah.

DAPHNE. All coding?

CHANTAL. Yeah. A bunch of paralegals running us around.

DAPHNE. Man.

ELAINE. Forty!

CHANTAL. I couldn't take it anymore.

ELAINE. It must've been a zoo.

CHANTAL. It was bad enough I was helping defend guys who made asbestos. Ooof. I couldn't I couldn't even get a week off for vacation! You'd think.

ELAINE. Yeah.

CHANTAL. So pfttt I quit.

ELAINE. What else are you gonna do?

BART. Pfttt.

CHANTAL. Split. Who got killed?

BART. Some guy.

DAPHNE. And some other guy.

BART. No.

DAPHNE. No?

BART. Some other woman.

DAPHNE. Naw.

BART. Yeah.

DAPHNE. Really?

BART. Yeah.

ELAINE. No one got killed.

BART. Yes.

ELAINE. No.

BART. A guy on the fourth floor.

ELAINE. A guy died. On the fourth floor.

CHANTAL. Some guy on the fourth floor got killed?

ELAINE. Died.

BART. Got killed.

DAPHNE. The other one wasn't another guy?

BART. No it was a woman.

DAPHNE. Oh.

ELAINE. Oh.

DAPHNE. Oh.

CHANTAL. Huh.

BART. Yeah.

ELAINE. No one got killed.

BART. That's not what Rick told me.

ELAINE. The newspaper said it was an accident.

BART. Or.

ELAINE. Or a suicide.

BART. The newspaper said it was an accident or a suicide.

ELAINE. Right.

BART. So they don't know.

ELAINE. Not a killing.

BART. They don't know.

ELAINE. Rick doesn't know either.

CHANTAL. How'd he die?

BART. The guy?

CHANTAL. Yeah.

DAPHNE. Are you sure about the woman?

BART. Yeah.

MARY. She worked on the sixteenth floor.

ELAINE. What?

DAPHNE. Who told you that?

BART. Where'd you hear that?

MARY. I was smoking with someone who works up there.

BART. Was it Tracy?

MARY. Who?

BART. Were you smoking with Tracy Was it Tracy?

MARY. It was a guy.

BART. What'd he say?

MARY. They found her and then the ambulance came.

BART. What else d'he say?

DAPHNE. Yeah?

MARY. That was it.

BART. That was it?

MARY. He works on the other side of the floor.

BART. That was it?

DAPHNE. Man.

BART. Two ambulances.

CHANTAL. In how long?

BART. Two weeks.

ELAINE. Three weeks.

BART. Two and a half. Thursday. Tuesday. Tuesday, today. Two and a half. When'd they find her?

MARY. What'd you mean?

BART. Was it in the morning or the afternoon?

MARY. I dunno.

BART. Ask him. The next time you. I wonder what happened to her.

DAPHNE. Bart?

BART. Because.

DAPHNE. Bart?

BART. I wonder if there was.

DAPHNE. Bart?

BART. Yeah?

DAPHNE. Can we not talk about it right now?

BART. Why not?

DAPHNE. I'm just getting.

BART. What?

DAPHNE. I just got this sick feeling.

ELAINE. Nobody got killed.

> (**CHANTAL** *opens her mouth wide.*
>
> **MARY** *has her head down.*)

BART. Oh.

> *(They are all silent.*
>
> **BART** *looks at all of the women.*)

BART. Oh yeah yeah yeah yeah ok.

> *(They are all silent.*
>
> *The elevator bell rings. They all start to work. The door opens and* **DIANE** *enters and sits down.*
>
> *They work at the tables in silence.* **DIANE** *stands up, adjusts her skirt. They all look. The lights go down slowly. Pale gray light to black.)*

Scene 5

(Lights up slowly. Lunch. **DAPHNE**, **BART**, **MARY** *and* **CHANTAL** *sit at the tables. Brown paper bags. Wax paper. Cans of soda.)*

DAPHNE. I'm not the easiest. I mean.

BART. Yeah you are.

DAPHNE. Naw I'm kind of. I can be, like, tight and sharp.

BART. So?

DAPHNE. So. He gets.

BART. He gets what?

DAPHNE. You know how Joey is.

BART. Yeah so what.

DAPHNE. It's raining so hard.

BART. Daphne.

DAPHNE. Look. The water's crashing down.

BART. Daphne.

DAPHNE. Joey doesn't

BART. What'd he do?

DAPHNE. So then he grabbed my arm.

BART. He did?

DAPHNE. No he didn't He was and then he sort of. Well. He.

BART. How?

DAPHNE. But it was my fault.

BART. Why?

DAPHNE. My boyfriend. Joey. He's. He works in a bank.

CHANTAL. Uh huh.

DAPHNE. I really love him.

BART. He's a Oh he's a good-looking guy.

DAPHNE. And he's smart.

BART. Yeah.

DAPHNE. He's smart.

BART. He is smart.

CHANTAL. Uh huh.

DAPHNE. And I think I love him.

CHANTAL. Uh huh.

DAPHNE. Most of the time.

CHANTAL. Uh huh.

DAPHNE. But sometimes. You know.

BART. How hard'd he grab your arm?

DAPHNE. Sometimes he's not. And I think.

CHANTAL. Uh huh.

DAPHNE. But. Then I see him and. *(Smiles.)*

CHANTAL. I had a guy like that.

BART. Me too.

DAPHNE. Yours work in a bank?

CHANTAL. No.

DAPHNE. Because it's stressful. It's.

BART. Still.

DAPHNE. He says all that money.

CHANTAL. Mine was a bartender. He made me smile like that.

DAPHNE. He gets stressed. And then I try to make him laugh. And sometimes that makes him.

CHANTAL. Uh huh.

DAPHNE. So.

CHANTAL. Mine broke my hand.

DAPHNE. *(Opens mouth wide. Closes it. Nonchalant.)* Huh.

BART. Uh huh.

DAPHNE. Ah.

BART. Uh huh.

DAPHNE. What did you.

CHANTAL. I had to look for new work.

DAPHNE. Oh.

CHANTAL. I couldn't type.

DAPHNE. No.

CHANTAL. My hand was broken.

BART. Did you?

DAPHNE. Did she what?

BART. Did you stay with him?

DAPHNE. Did you?

CHANTAL. Yeah.

DAPHNE. You did?

CHANTAL. For a while.

BART. So did I.

MARY. Half the plants in the world are gonna be gone in eighty years.

DAPHNE. What?

MARY. Extinct. Gone.

DAPHNE. What?

MARY. Plus there won't be any fish left. In the ocean.

DAPHNE. Why'd you stay with him?

CHANTAL. He'd make me smile.

BART. Right.

CHANTAL. And I'd forget.

BART. I stayed with mine too.

CHANTAL. Uh huh.

BART. Until I couldn't.

CHANTAL. It kind of creeped up on me.

BART. Yeah. I didn't really notice.

CHANTAL. And then.

DAPHNE. Who was that Bart?

BART. What?

DAPHNE. Which guy are you talking about?

BART. Daphne I'm just saying you just got to be careful.

DAPHNE. Joey wouldn't.

BART. You just gotta.

DAPHNE. I don't gotta anything.

BART. Daphne. I'm.

DAPHNE. Joey's. *(Turns red.)*

BART. I'm

DAPHNE. *(Tight mouth.)*

BART. I'm going up to the sixteenth floor. I'm going to ask my friend Tracy about that woman.

(Waits for elevator. Goes.)

DAPHNE. Joey wouldn't do that.

CHANTAL. That's good.

DAPHNE. I wouldn't let him.

CHANTAL. Uh huh.

DAPHNE. It's hard because his job is hard. Like, I wouldn't want to do it. All that. Money. He comes home and.

CHANTAL. It was weird. I got.

I felt like I was a. A piece of wood after. I felt.

MARY. It's hard being scared.

(Pause.)

CHANTAL. Yeah.

(Pause.)

MARY. Yeah.

(Pause.)

CHANTAL. Yeah.

And it's hard not to be.

(Pause.)

MARY. Yeah.

CHANTAL. Even now. Sometimes I. Just stop. And look. Around.

MARY. People are always scaring us.

DAPHNE. I'm not going to be.

CHANTAL. Good. Because.

MARY. Everywhere all the time. WATCH OUT FOR THIS! WATCH OUT FOR THAT!

CHANTAL. That's good.

DAPHNE. He'd have to.

CHANTAL. Good.

> *(Pause.)*

MARY. I wonder if it's going to stop raining.

> *(Lightning. Crash of thunder.)*

MARY *(laughs.)* I guess not.

> *(Laughs.*
>
> *Laughs again.)*

DAPHNE. You used to type?

CHANTAL. I did that for a long time.

DAPHNE. I've never typed.

CHANTAL. No?

DAPHNE. It bugs me.

CHANTAL. I liked it. I used to get lost in it.

DAPHNE. I hate those typing tests.

CHANTAL. Yeah.

DAPHNE. They want you to go fast.

CHANTAL. Yeah they.

DAPHNE. You do them and you get all blurry.

CHANTAL. Huh.

DAPHNE. You wanna pass out.

CHANTAL. They take concentration.

DAPHNE. They bug me.

CHANTAL. Sounds like.

DAPHNE. I get fired all the time.

CHANTAL. You do?

DAPHNE. Yeah. I don't care.

CHANTAL. Keeps things exciting.

DAPHNE. Yeah!

MARY. *(Laughs.)* People make me laugh.

CHANTAL. Why?

MARY. They just do.

DAPHNE. One place told me my hair was too big.

CHANTAL. What?

DAPHNE. This girl she was all "Your hair's too big for the city."

CHANTAL. Really?

DAPHNE. Yeah.

CHANTAL. Did she want you to cut it?

DAPHNE. Naw. She fired me.

MARY. Oh boy.

CHANTAL. Because of your hair?

DAPHNE. They had a very little office.
Plus I was too slow.

CHANTAL. Huh.

DAPHNE. She was like "Maybe in Arizona" cause that's where I am from originally Arizona "Maybe in Arizona there's room but there's not enough room here in the city for hair like that, plus you're too slow."
I didn't care.

CHANTAL. I've been fired.

MARY. Oh boy.

DAPHNE. I worked at a place It's sister company was El Paso Gas so of course you laugh.

CHANTAL. El Paso Gas?

DAPHNE. Yeah. In El Paso. In Texas.

CHANTAL. You laughed?

DAPHNE. Of course I laughed. Who'd name a gas company that? El Paso Gas!

CHANTAL. They didn't think it was funny?

DAPHNE. No.

MARY. You'd call it Texas Gas.

DAPHNE. Yeah. Or. Something else.

MARY. Yeah.

DAPHNE. They fired me. Plus I was too slow.

MARY. Or El Paso Resources.

DAPHNE. I don't know how I keep this job.

MARY. Diane likes you.

DAPHNE. Yeah.

CHANTAL. She does?

DAPHNE. Yeah. And Elaine.

MARY. She likes you too. And you're never late.

DAPHNE. Yeah.

MARY. And you never miss a day.

DAPHNE. I have perfect attendance.

CHANTAL. I thought you don't like work.

DAPHNE. I like being at work. I just don't like working.
It bugs me.
You got to stay on their good side. Diane and Elaine.

MARY. Yeah.

DAPHNE. And you got to watch out for Mercedes.

MARY. Yeah.

CHANTAL. You do?

MARY. She turns people in.

CHANTAL. She does?

MARY. Halpert's always calling her downstairs.

DAPHNE. She's his favorite.

MARY. Yeah.

DAPHNE. Watch out for her.

MARY. We don't.

DAPHNE. Yeah we don't.

CHANTAL. What?

DAPHNE. We don't. Get too involved with her.

CHANTAL. Oh.

MARY. She'll take you down.

DAPHNE. Yeah.

MARY. She will take you down. Down!

DAPHNE. Watch out for her.

MARY. Watch out for Elaine.

CHANTAL. Yeah?

MARY. Oh! Yeah.

DAPHNE. Yeah.

MARY. She can be.

   (Gestures.)

DAPHNE. Yup.

MARY. She's crazy.

DAPHNE. Yeah.

CHANTAL. Really?

MARY. Yeah really crazy.

DAPHNE. Like crazy crazy.

MARY. Be careful.

DAPHNE. Yeah.

MARY. Some days she's ok.

DAPHNE. And then.

MARY. Somedays.

   (Gestures.)

DAPHNE. Crazy!

MARY. Yeah.

DAPHNE. Yeah.

MARY. Yeah.

CHANTAL. Ok.

MARY. Diane's mostly ok.

CHANTAL. Yeah?

DAPHNE. Yeah.

MARY. Yeah.

CHANTAL. Thanks.

MARY. Mostly.

DAPHNE. Yeah. And Bart's ok.

MARY. Yeah.

CHANTAL. Thanks.

DAPHNE. Sure.

MARY. Yeah.

DAPHNE. And we're ok.

MARY. *(Laughs.)* Mostly!

DAPHNE. Except I don't like working!

CHANTAL. *(Laughs.)*

DAPHNE. It bugs me!

MARY. Watch out for Mercedes.

CHANTAL. Ok.

MARY. Just make sure you.

CHANTAL. I usually don't. Get too.

DAPHNE. What'd you bring for lunch?

CHANTAL. A sandwich.

DAPHNE. Oh.

MARY. Oh.

CHANTAL. And some chips.

DAPHNE. Oh.

MARY. I love chips.

CHANTAL. I ate them.

MARY. I love chips.

CHANTAL. Next time I'll.

MARY. Oh no I don't eat them.

CHANTAL. Oh.

MARY. I love them though.

(*Elevator bells rings.* **JOEY** *enters.*)

DAPHNE. Joey?

JOEY. Hey Daph.

DAPHNE. Joey what are you. Hi.

JOEY. Thought I'd come say hi.

DAPHNE. That was nice of you.

JOEY. Yeah well.

(*He goes to kiss her.*)

DAPHNE. Joey!

JOEY. I came to give you a kiss.

DAPHNE. Joey. It's the office.

JOEY. Yeah so?

DAPHNE. You're crazy.

JOEY. Uh huh? Hey.

DAPHNE. This is my boyfriend Joey.

JOEY. Hey.

CHANTAL. Hello Joey.

JOEY. Hey.

DAPHNE. You have lunch?

JOEY. Yeah.

DAPHNE. What'd you have?

JOEY. Which table you working at today?

DAPHNE. Over there. Me and Bart switched.

JOEY. Yeah?

DAPHNE. I got bored.

CHANTAL. Where do you work?

JOEY. Downtown.

DAPHNE. He's got, like, a good job.

JOEY. So you got the.

DAPHNE. Got the what?

JOEY. You know.

DAPHNE. What Joey?

JOEY. You know Daphne.

DAPHNE. No. No.

JOEY. Why not?

DAPHNE. I told you.

JOEY. *(Laughs.)* Daphne.

DAPHNE. What.

JOEY. You'll have to excuse us.

CHANTAL. Ok sure.

JOEY. Daphne.

DAPHNE. You're going to be late.

JOEY. No I'm not.

DAPHNE. How long's your lunch.

JOEY. I can.

DAPHNE. Mine's almost over. So I better.

JOEY. You gotta do what I want you to do.

DAPHNE. No I don't.

JOEY. Yeah. You do.

DAPHNE. I don't have. Joey.

JOEY. You're always.

DAPHNE. Joey come on.

JOEY. Why can't you? Can't you ever just.

DAPHNE. Why don't you do it yourself?

JOEY. You're worthless It's worthless talking to you about

DAPHNE. I'm what?

JOEY. You're being a problem Daphne.

DAPHNE. I am?

JOEY. Yeah.

DAPHNE. Oh, like, you're

JOEY. Yeah.

DAPHNE. Huh.

JOEY. I got to give it to Bobby and I have to give it to him soon so you got to He's not that excited to

DAPHNE. That's your problem.

JOEY. No.

DAPHNE. Yeah.

JOEY. No. It's your problem too Daphne.

DAPHNE. It is not.

JOEY. Yeah because he thinks.

DAPHNE. What does he think?

JOEY. He thinks it's your problem too.

DAPHNE. Oh great Joey That's great.

JOEY. That's what he.

DAPHNE. Great.

JOEY. So you.

DAPHNE. Stop it.

JOEY. What?

DAPHNE. Don't touch me.

JOEY. I'm going to touch you if I want to.

DAPHNE. No you're.

JOEY. I'm your boyfriend.

DAPHNE. I told you Joey I told you I wasn't going to.

JOEY. Yeah you are.

DAPHNE. No I'm not.

JOEY. Jesus.

DAPHNE. Yeah. Jesus.

JOEY. Look. Look. Look.

DAPHNE. Look at what.

JOEY. I was going to say sorry about yesterday but you're

DAPHNE. Joey Joey

JOEY. *(Fast and low and hard.)* But I'm not sorry because you because you because you And that that that You understand me Daphne Do you? Do you?

>*(**DAPHNE** turns. **JOEY** grabs **DAPHNE** from behind. An echo of the statue of Daphne and Apollo by Bernini. Broken when the elevator bell rings.)*

DAPHNE. *(Quietly.)* Ow. Joey. Ow.

>*(**BART** enters.)*

BART. Oh. Hey Joey.

JOEY. Hey.

>*(**BART** sneezes.)*

DAPHNE. Bless you.

JOEY. Yeah.

BART. Thank you.

JOEY. So.

>*(**BART** sneezes.)*

DAPHNE. Bless you.

BART. Thank you Were you just leaving?

JOEY. Yeah.

BART. Oh.

JOEY. Yeah.

BART. Oh. Ok. Ok. So.

JOEY. I'll see you later Daphne.

DAPHNE. Yeah.

JOEY. Yeah.

> (*Gets on elevator. Exits.*
>
> **BART** *sneezes.*)

DAPHNE. Bless you.

BART. (*Pulls candy out of his pockets.*) They have so much candy on the sixteenth floor. It's beautiful up there.

DAPHNE. What'd your friend say?

BART. It's like bliss.

DAPHNE. Yeah?

BART. They have free sodas.

DAPHNE. They do?

BART. They have free sodas and tons of candy.

DAPHNE. Lucky!

BART. Free sodas I feel kind of sick.

DAPHNE. I'll take that. (*Takes candy.*)

BART. But kind of a blissful sick.

DAPHNE. Oh my god purple lick sticks yum yum yum!

BART. You should see how many phone lines Tracy does.

CHANTAL. What did she say about that woman?

BART. She didn't She didn't know her really well.

DAPHNE. Oh.

BART. But she died in the hall.

CHANTAL. In the hall?

BART. At the end of the hall.

DAPHNE. Really?

BART. Around this little corner I guess. And I guess there was blood.

All the lights in their stairwells are busted.

DAPHNE. Really?

BART. Yeah, they're busted. You'd think.

DAPHNE. Call, like, maintenance.

BART. That's what I told Tracy.

DAPHNE. This place is a dump.

BART. You'd think.

DAPHNE. Makes me crazy. They got all this money.

BART. You'd frigging think.

Don't eat all those. You'll feel really sick.

(Elevator bell rings. **DIANE** *and* **ELAINE** *enter.* **DIANE** *doesn't hear the following.)*

ELAINE. *(Whispered.)* Police.

BART. *(Whispered.)* What?

ELAINE. *(Whispered.)* Police.

DAPHNE. *(Whispered.)* What?

BART. *(Whispered.)* Police.

DAPHNE. *(Whispered.)* What?

*(***BART** *nods.)*

DAPHNE. *(Whispered.)* No shit.

CHANTAL. *(Whispered.)* What?

DAPHNE. *(Whispered.)* Police.

CHANTAL. *(Whispered.)* What?

DAPHNE. *(Whispered.)* Yeah.

CHANTAL. *(Whispered.)* Police?

MARY. *(Whispered.)* What?

CHANTAL. *(Whispered.)* Police.

MARY. *(Whispered.)* Oh. Oh.

DIANE. Let's get to work.

(They are all silent.

They work at the tables in silence. The lights go down slowly. Pale gray light to black.)

Scene 6

(Elevator bell rings. Lights up quickly. **MERCEDES** *enters.)*

MERCEDES. It's. I'm. This. For that whole time! And. It's. I'm. You'd. I even missed my lunch so I. Because. I'm. This this this this.

DIANE. What?

MERCEDES. I'm.

(**MERCEDES** *goes offstage to the bathroom.*

They all look around.)

BART. Huh.

DIANE. Yeah.

DAPHNE. What was that all about?

DIANE. Let's just let's just let's just keep working.

DAPHNE. *(Rising.)* Should I?

DIANE. No I think. Let's just let her.

DAPHNE. But she.

DIANE. That's just Mercedes.

(**MERCEDES** *enters.)*

MERCEDES. That was that was that was I'm very.

DIANE. Are you ok?

MERCEDES. I'm upset.

DIANE. You sound.

MERCEDES. The police. They're interviewing people. In the building!

BART. Who?

DIANE. Bart.

BART. I just want to.

DAPHNE. Because of the rumors?

DIANE. Ok you guys.

MERCEDES. I'd like to go home.

DIANE. Mercedes.

MERCEDES. I think.

DIANE. I don't think.

MERCEDES. Mr Halpert. I guess he. He gave them my name. Which is.

BART. The police?

DAPHNE. Why'd he give'm your name?

MERCEDES. I don't know!

BART. Do they think you?

DAPHNE. They don't think you.

MERCEDES. I'd like to go home.

DIANE. I'm not sure you.

MERCEDES. I'd like to.

DIANE. I don't think Mr. Halpert would be ok.

ELAINE. Why were the police?

MERCEDES. They were asking us about that guy.

ELAINE. They were?

DIANE. Ok.

BART. I knew it!

ELAINE. What?

BART. I knew it!

DIANE. Bart.

BART. I knew something was!

MERCEDES. Yeah!

DIANE. Ok.

DAPHNE. Oh.

DIANE. Ok.

BART. Man.

DAPHNE. Oh.

ELAINE. Why were they?

BART. Because something did.

DIANE. Ok. OK.

Mercedes. Sit down.

MERCEDES. I want to go home.

DIANE. Just.

Mercedes. Sit down.

MERCEDES. I don't want to sit down.

DIANE. For a moment.

MERCEDES. Because why else would they?

BART. There must be some.

DIANE. All I know is.

MERCEDES. Diane what if.

DIANE. Mercedes all I know is. Mr. Halpert wouldn't.

MERCEDES. I'm I'm.

DIANE. Do you want to come back?

MERCEDES. Diane.

DIANE. Do you?

MERCEDES. Diane.

DIANE. Do you?

MERCEDES. Yes.

DIANE. So.

(*Pause.*)

You know he's.

MERCEDES. I know.

DIANE. So.

MERCEDES. They had a few of us sitting in a room. No one knows what's going on.

MARY. Maybe nothing.

DIANE. Right.

MERCEDES. I waited and waited and waited and waited and waited and then they talked to me and I said "I don't know anything" and then they said "Ok thank you" and then I was done and they let me come back up here.

MARY. Maybe nothing's going on.

MERCEDES. And no one else knew anything. They had a lot of papers.

MARY. This whole thing.

DIANE. Mary's right.

MERCEDES. And no one would tell me anything.

MARY. In Brunswick In Maine In Brunswick ok maybe every
five years or so maybe ok, something would happen
and the whole town would. And it could be terrible.
But in this. But. But. But in this city there's so much.

DAPHNE. Didn't anyone?

MARY. And then TV and the news the news the news again
and again and the papers and the internet and I'm
It's everywhere all the time.

(Everyone is quiet.)

We're not supposed to hear all this. We're not. We're
not. Not all this. All these disasters from close and
from far away. We're always. Everybody's always always
always on edge.

And maybe nothing.

But my heart is always in. It's always in. In my throat.

(Everyone is quiet.)

Aw crap.

(She breathes in fast.)

BART. *(laughs.)*

MARY. *(pops her lips.)* So let's get back to work.

DIANE. Right.

MERCEDES. A guy I was sitting with while I waited and
waited said we better be careful.

BART. Who?

MERCEDES. The people on our floor.

DIANE. Mercedes.

BART. Why?

DIANE. Let's talk about this later.

CHANTAL. Why?

DIANE. Right now let's.

MERCEDES. He said we should leave.

DAPHNE. Why?

BART. Who said this?

DIANE. We're not leaving.

BART. Why he say that?

DIANE. Let's get back to work.

MERCEDES. The woman who runs the stinky store might be missing.

(Pause.)

BART. Man.

CHANTAL. She might be missing?

DAPHNE. It was shut The store was shut.

CHANTAL. What do you mean missing?

BART. Who said this?

MERCEDES. Someone just said.

DIANE. Ok that's enough.

DAPHNE. She might be missing?

CHANTAL. Missing how?

MERCEDES. Someone said.

DAPHNE. Like missing missing?

DIANE. Let's get back.

MERCEDES. And he said. First floor.

BART. What?

CHANTAL. So?

MERCEDES. The stinky store is on the first floor.

BART. Yeah so?

CHANTAL. So?

DIANE. That's enough Mercedes.

MERCEDES. That guy that was killed was from the fourth floor.

DIANE. He wasn't killed!

ELAINE. So?

MERCEDES. And that woman.

ELAINE. What about her?

DIANE. Elaine.

MERCEDES. She was from the sixteenth floor.

ELAINE. So?

DIANE. Elaine.

MERCEDES. One. Four. Sixteen.

DIANE. Oh one four sixteen yeah so.

BART. Yeah so what?

MERCEDES. We're on the ninth floor.

DIANE. Fine So what Mercedes.

MERCEDES. One times one is one. Two times two is four.

   (Pause.)

BART. So?

MERCEDES. So four times four is sixteen.

ELAINE. Four times four is sixteen.

MERCEDES. Right.

BART. Four times four is sixteen.

ELAINE. One times one Two times two Four times four.

MERCEDES. Right.

CHANTAL. Uh huh.

MERCEDES. Right. See?

DAPHNE. What? See?

BART. Oh. Oh.

DAPHNE. See what?

BART. Three times three.

MERCEDES. We're on the ninth floor. Right?

DAPHNE. So what?

ELAINE. Three times three.

MERCEDES. Is nine.

DAPHNE. Oh come on.

MERCEDES. It is.

DAPHNE. That's stupid. That's stupid.

BART. I dunno.

DAPHNE. One four sixteen. Pffft. Stupid.

BART. Anyone want any candy? I've got a bunch of.

MERCEDES. We're on the ninth floor.

DIANE. That's right Mercedes. We're on the ninth floor.

DAPHNE. We are. We're on the ninth floor! Pffft.

MERCEDES. So I think. I think.

DIANE. I think you've done plenty of thinking.

ELAINE. Diane.

BART. I think.

DAPHNE. Stupid.

CHANTAL. Um.

DIANE. No ok. We've got piles

(**MERCEDES** *opens her mouth.*)

No. No no no no uh uh no. Listen.

That's enough.

Mercedes sit down. Because I WILL tell Halpert.

I'll!

(*They are all silent.*)

Jesus goddamn it!

(*They sit at the tables in silence.*)

I don't want to hear another peep out of anyone.

(*Pause.*

Pause.

Pause.)

BART. Peep.

DIANE. Oh you're in big trouble mister.

(*Lights very suddenly to black. The stage is black until noted. It is raining hard outside, black sky.*

All together react:)

MERCEDES. (*Screams.*)

DAPHNE. (*Squeak.*)

MARY. (*Gasp.*)

BART. OH.

CHANTAL. Um.

ELAINE. Um um um.

    (A flicker pause; then:)

DIANE. That's not funny That's not FUNNY. So whoever.

ELAINE. SH.

DIANE. What sh?

ELAINE. SH.

    (Silence.)

DIANE. The lights are out. The lights are just out.

MARY. The whole block is out. Look.

ELAINE. SH.

DIANE. Stop saying sh. The lights are just.

ELAINE. SH. I think I

MERCEDES. I'm I'm I'm I'm

BART. Man.

DAPHNE. Bart?

BART. What?

DAPHNE. So the elevator?

BART. It's not gonna work.

DIANE. I'm calling the building. I'm going to find out.

CHANTAL. We should of gone home.

MERCEDES. I'm I'm I'm.

DIANE. Everybody just. I'm calling the.

ELAINE. Sh. I keep hearing.

BART. What do you? Is that Elaine?

ELAINE. I think there's someone

BART. It's probably

    (We hear heavy breathing.)

ELAINE. That! That. SH.

CHANTAL. What's that?

BART. What is.

MERCEDES. *(Whimpers.)*

BART. Who is that?

DAPHNE. Hey! Who is

DIANE. I'm calling the police. I'm I'm on the I'm

CHANTAL. *(Whispered)* Where's it coming from?

BART. I don't.

DAPHNE. Bart.

> *(Lightning flashes.*
>
> *Thunder.)*

BART. Ah ah.

MERCEDES. *(Moans.)*

DAPHNE. Um um.

ELAINE. I hear a scratching

CHANTAL. *(Breathes in fast.)*

> *(Lightning flashes.*
>
> *Thunder.*
>
> *Someone is in front of the window.*
>
> *At once:*
>
> *A door slams.*
>
> *Heavy breathing.*
>
> *A chair scrapes across the floor.*
>
> *Something crashes.*
>
> **MERCEDES** *screams.* **BART** *shouts.*
>
> *Someone screams and runs down the hall offstage.*
>
> *The rain crashes down.*
>
> *Someone slams through the stairwell door, runs down the stairs.*
>
> *We hear the person trip, scream, crash down the stairs. A heavy thud as the person hits.*
>
> *We hear heavy breathing.)*

CHANTAL. Who was that? Who was?

> *(Flicker silence. Then fast:)*

CHANTAL. Who screamed? Who?

DAPHNE. Not me.

DIANE. Who was that?

DAPHNE. Not me.

CHANTAL. Not me.

BART. Not me.

DIANE. Who is that?

DAPHNE. Daphne.

DIANE. Bart?

BART. Yeah?

DIANE. Let's go and

BART. Let's go check.

DAPHNE. Go

BART. Yeah yeah

DIANE. Yeah

BART. Yeah yeah ok yeah Let's

> (**BART** *and* **DIANE** *check the offstage stairwell; we hear:*)

DIANE. Oh oh oh no

BART. Oh no

> (*They run down the offstage stairs.*)

DIANE. Oh my God. Oh my God she's Oh my God

BART. She's

> (**DIANE** *runs up the stairs and onstage to find the phone.*)

DIANE. Oh no. Oh no. She's.

CHANTAL. Who was?

MERCEDES. What what what

DIANE. Where's the goddamn Where's the goddamn

CHANTAL. What

DAPHNE. Diane what do you

DIANE. Goddamn Goddamn

CHANTAL. Who was?

MERCEDES. I'm I'm I'm

DIANE. *(On phone.)* Yeah Someone's

Someone's really hurt up here, in the stairs In the stairs
in the stairs

Between the eighth and ninth I don't know. I think
she's

MERCEDES. Who?

CHANTAL. Oh my God who

*(Lights flash on and then off again. We see a flash of
the stage.)*

MERCEDES. Oh!

*(Again. Lights flash on and then off again. Again. We
see a flash of the stage. Almost a freeze frame.)*

MERCEDES. Oh.

(Lights come on.)

BART. It was Elaine She's.

*(***BART*** and ***ELAINE*** enter. Her right arm is broken and
awkward. There is blood on her face; her nose is broken.
She carries the pieces of her glasses in her left hand.)*

MERCEDES. Oh

CHANTAL. What's

BART. I think her arm's.

DIANE. Don't move her You should have

BART. I'm pretty sure her arm's

ELAINE. I broke my glasses. I broke my glasses.

BART. Look her arm's It's really really

DIANE. You shouldn't have moved her Get her to the

CHANTAL. Get her a

DIANE. It's going You're going to Oh my God Elaine.

ELAINE. I broke my glasses I'm not going to be able to
work

BART. Ok ok ok ok

CHANTAL. It's really.

DAPHNE. She's

DIANE. *(Breath catches in her throat.)*

DAPHNE. She's.

DIANE. I don't know what we should They're sending some. They're coming up here.

MERCEDES. I want to go home.

MARY. *(Looks at rain.)*

DIANE. Someone's coming up here. It's going to be

CHANTAL. I'm cold.

BART. I am too.

CHANTAL. It's cold in here.

BART. Put on your coat.

CHANTAL. I'm cold.

MERCEDES. Did someone push you down the stairs?

DIANE. What?

MERCEDES. Did someone

DIANE. You didn't just

MERCEDES. Maybe someone

CHANTAL. Oh.

DIANE. You ridiculous. You stupid stupid

MERCEDES. I heard You all heard

DIANE. Stupid stupid

MERCEDES. I heard

DIANE. You pushed her down the stairs!

CHANTAL. She was just.

MERCEDES. What?

DIANE. You did! Mercedes! You did!

MERCEDES. Diane.

DIANE. You did!

MERCEDES. I didn't! I.

BART. Diane.

DIANE. All of you! Did! You pushed her! You!

(Silence.)

MERCEDES. I want to go home.

DIANE. *(Opens eyes wide.)*

MERCEDES. You should have let me go home. Then

DIANE. Oh

BART. Diane.

MERCEDES. You should have let me go home!

DAPHNE. I don't want to go home. Joey's at. I'm scared to go home. I don't want.

(She sits at a table in her coat.

Lights go down slowly. Pale grey light to black.)

Scene 7

(Lights come up slowly. Later that evening. **DAPHNE** *sits at one of the tables. She wears her coat. The noises in the office.*

Lights go down slowly. Pale grey light to black.)

Scene 8

(Lights come up slowly. The next morning. The noises in the office.

Elevator bell. **MERCEDES** *enters. She takes off her coat. She exits into the kitchen and makes the coffee. She enters. Stands. Looks back into the kitchen. Sits. Waits.*

Waits. Mutters. Waits.

Noises in the office.

Elevator bell. **DIANE** *enters.)*

MERCEDES. Oh. Ah!

*(***DIANE*** *looks at* **MERCEDES**. *Goes to her seat. Takes off her coat. Exits into the kitchen. Enters with coffee. Sits.*

Elevator bell. **BART** *enters.)*

MERCEDES. Bart. Hi Bart.

BART. Hi.

Hi Diane.

DIANE. Good morning.

BART. Good morning.

MERCEDES. I made the Um

*(***BART*** *exits into the kitchen.* **MERCEDES** *stands. Sits.*

BART *enters. Sits.)*

DIANE. Is it nine?

MERCEDES. Almost. No. Almost. I think. No.

DIANE. Ok.

(They sit.)

MERCEDES. Um.

*(***DIANE*** *looks at some papers.)*

MERCEDES. My bus missed its exit. This morning.

DIANE. That new woman. Chantal? Who was here yesterday? She's not coming back in.

MERCEDES. She isn't?

DIANE. No.

MERCEDES. Oh.

BART. Well you wouldn't.

MERCEDES. Oh. Kkk.

DIANE. No.

BART. I mean, I wouldn't.

(Silence.)

DIANE. Mr. Halpert will send someone else up.

MERCEDES. Oh.

DIANE. To take her place.

(Silence.)

DIANE. So.

(Silence.

Elevator bell. **MARY** *enters. Crosses to her chair.)*

DIANE. Good morning Mary.

(Pause.)

Good morning Mary.

MARY. Oh. Yeah. Good morning.

MERCEDES. Hi Mary.

BART. Hey Mary.

MARY. Hi. Hi Bart.

DIANE. So I think it's nine. So let's.
First though Before we get started We need
We can't eat lunch in this room any more.

BART. What?

MERCEDES. Really? Why?

DIANE. No. I've been asked to tell you they'd prefer it if
we ate our lunches outside the office from now on.
So. I'm going to pass this paper around. You need to
put your initials next to your name. So they know you
heard me tell you no more lunch in the office.

BART. Why?

DIANE. Just initial it Bart.

MERCEDES. That's.

DIANE. Well that's just. Put your initials here Mercedes.

MERCEDES. Where?

DIANE. Here. Here.

MERCEDES. *(Opens eyes wide.)*

DIANE. Mary.

Ok.

So. It's nine.

BART. Where's Daphne?

DIANE. It's nine Bart. Let's. Just.

(Lights go down slowly. Pale grey light to black. **MERCEDES**, **BART**, **MARY** *and* **DIANE** *work at the tables. The noises in the office. Lights go down slowly. Pale grey light to black.)*

FINAL BLACKOUT

OTHER TITLES AVAILABLE FROM SAMUEL FRENCH

THE DRUNKEN CITY

Adam Bock

Comedy / 3m, 3f

Off on the bar crawl to end all crawls, three twenty-something brides-to-be find their lives going topsy-turvy when one of them begins to question her future after a chance encounter with a recently jilted handsome stranger. *The Drunken City* is a wildly theatrical take on the mystique of marriage and the ever-shifting nature of love and identity in a city that never sleeps

"A playful and hopeful comedy. Like the best episodes of 'Sex and the City,' a little heartache always goes well with hilarity. The cast is appealing, adorable, and top-shelf. There's only one response to something as pleasing as *The Drunken City* - another round!"
– *New York Daily News*

"A lot of fun! Adam Bock's scalpel-sharp insight has made him a potent force on today's theater scene. Trip Cullman pitches the performances at just the right level of wooziness. Tart, smart and intoxicating."
– *The New York Sun*

OTHER TITLES AVAILABLE FROM SAMUEL FRENCH

EURYDICE

Sarah Ruhl

Dramatic Comedy, 5m, 2f / Unit Set

In *Eurydice*, Sarah Ruhl reimagines the classic myth of Orpheus through the eyes of its heroine. Dying too young on her wedding day, Eurydice must journey to the underworld, where she reunites with her father and struggles to remember her lost love. With contemporary characters, ingenious plot twists, and breathtaking visual effects, the play is a fresh look at a timeless love story.

"RHAPSODICALLY BEAUTIFUL. A weird and wonderful new play - an inexpressibly moving theatrical fable about love, loss and the pleasures and pains of memory."
– *The New York Times*

"EXHILARATING!! A luminous retelling of the Orpheus myth, lush and limpid as a dream where both author and audience swim in the magical, sometimes menacing, and always thrilling flow of the unconscious."
– *The New Yorker*

"Exquisitely staged by Les Waters and an inventive design team… Ruhl's wild flights of imagination, some deeply affecting passages and beautiful imagery provide transporting pleasures. They conspire to create original, at times breathtaking, stage pictures."
– *Variety*

"Touching, inventive, invigoratingly compact and luminously liquid in its rhythms and design, "Eurydice" reframes the ancient myth of ill-fated love to focus not on the bereaved musician but on his dead bride – and on her struggle with love beyond the grave as both wife and daughter."
– *The San Francisco Chronicle*